REVENGE IS JUSTICE

PX DUKE

Jim Nash Read Order

Marina Mystery	Revenge Is Justice
Twisted Sisters	Escape
Sleeping with a .45	Wedding Bell Blues
Pirate Cay	Breakdown
Thrill Kill Jill	Little Girl Lost
Greetings From Key West	Forget Me Not
Lost Paradise	All The Glitter
No Angels	Mexico Time
Mexico Gamble	Partners In Crime
No Picnic	Shop Till You Drop
Fallen Angels	Lobo
Vendetta	No Free Ride
A Girl's Best Friend	Gone
Dead End	Stealing America
No Harbor	Blame It on Djibouti
Dog Days	No Escape
Startup Blues	Trouble in Paradise
Last Stop to Nowhere / The Last Goodbye	

SEASONAL

Trick or Treat

Helping Santa

OTHER

The Snap Brim Fedora Caper

The Lady in White

The Lady in Yellow

Print books

Jim Nash

Jim Nash The Beginning
Gun Crazy
Gun Crazy 2
Gun Crazy 3
Fallen Angels
Last Stop to Nowhere / The Last Goodbye
Revenge Is Justice
Escape / Forget Me Not
Wedding Bell Blues / Breakdown
Mexico Time
Lobo
No Free Ride / Gone

Harry Delaney Adventures

Dead Reckoning
Uncharted
Go-Around
Sand Storm

Frank Ross Biker Tales

No Way Out
Bank Robber Dames
Bad Girls

Other

The Last President

REVENGE
IS JUSTICE

And if you wrong us shall we not revenge?
– William Shakespeare

1

Jim Nash strolled down the stairs from his second-floor office and out onto the sidewalk. He hesitated at the curb before looking both ways. Waited for a car to go by before stepping off the curb. Hands slipped into pockets, and he casually made his way across the street. He reached the opposite sidewalk, turned, and looked back the way he came. His eyes traveled up to the second floor of the office building.

Two women, illuminated by a neon sign in a window, looked down and waved.

DAWSON & NASH - INVESTIGATORS

He purposefully chose the single last word. He didn't want to use *Detective Agency*, or *Private Detectives*, or put some other word in front of it. That one word, *Investigators*, made it sound hands-off. As though whoever stopped by might only take a look, or want to make inquiries, or maybe ask a question or two before moving on.

He returned the wave and headed for Burrito

Heaven. Miraculously, both women loved the place almost as much as he did.

It was the women who convinced him to buy the sign. His partners. Neither licensed as investigators. It took some talking to get them to promise to work toward their licenses. Bobbie Dawson was already in the process. He found Andrea Sharpe working full time as a bartender while she made payments on the university degree she got at MIT.

It took Andrea five long years in the accelerated program, but she graduated with a *summa cum laude* or its equivalent PhD in some obscure science that she declined to put into practice. Perhaps just as well she couldn't find a job in her field. It meant she worked part time for him after he twisted her arm and her affection in too many directions.

Andrea argued against his offer of a second job when he approached her. Shift work at the small bar down the street was taking up most of her time and effort. The tips weren't bad, either.

She made it plain that all his business needed was a sharp pencil and a notepad to go with it. Maybe a roll of quarters and a pay phone, the woman had added, almost as an afterthought.

He had grinned and looked right at her. "You're just the sharp pencil I need. With the dearth of pay phones these days, you can forgo the trip to the bank for the roll of change."

She laughed and accepted on the spot.

Andrea didn't know him well. She might have thought he was just another drunk she helped sober up. His drinking forced her to come between an intoxicated Jim and two of her regulars. From what she later told him, they took exception to his drunken ways in her bar. She took away his keys, allowed him into her home, and put him to bed, where she made sure he slept it off.

That she had to confiscate his car keys was no small matter for either of them.

As payment, he cooked a breakfast he needed to go out and buy in order to stock the woman's fridge. When he asked for a favor, as though that might repay her kindness toward him, she agreed before knowing the full story.

Silly me, he recalled her telling him when she learned she was riding in a 60-year-old convertible on her way to rescue his latest girlfriend from an air boat escapade in the everglades.

Bobbie Dawson and Andrea Sharpe hit it off, and, apprehensive as he was at first, he was glad of it. He found himself with two employees he could trust without question. Andrea kept her job in the bar, albeit with reduced hours, and lost the boyfriend, also a bartender in the place.

From four to nine p.m. most evenings, Andrea kept watch over the office before heading off to her late shift. She forwarded texts and messages and generally kept office spirits up when clients didn't line up to knock on the door.

It was working out. The women got along. He liked them both—although he loved Bobbie. He even thought he might tell her, too—when he found the right time.

He ended his reminiscing when he arrived at Burrito Heaven. He picked up three to go with coffee and headed back to the office on the opposite side of the street. He recalled how, at first, Andrea was reluctant to sample the burritos until Bobbie related the story of how she met him. A northern girl, she tried one, and fell in like with the spicy wrap.

Breakfast burritos became a constant shared by the three partners.

Jim paused to listen before pushing the office door open. He caught out the women talking about office improvements. So much for the budget, and they'd only just refurbished the place.

"All right, you two. You're getting along far too well if you're thinking I'll spend more money on this dump."

He looked around at the expensive, avant-garde furniture. They all pitched in to make the place smell of fresh paint and cleaning supplies. He objected to the cost of it all, but in the end, he came around. After all, their new digs were in an expensive area of Magic City. They insisted he had to keep up appearances to fit in with what they hoped would be a better class of clientele.

"Jimbo, you just pay the bills. We'll take it from there," they reassured him.

He paid, and they did.

Andrea took to calling him Jimbo almost from the moment they met. It was ages since he heard anyone use that nickname. He didn't mind. He liked Andrea. Maybe a little too much for anyone's good. Especially his own.

"Which reminds me, boss." Andrea looked across at Bobbie, unsure if she should continue. Bobbie only nodded, and Andrea went on. "Someone left a really weird voice mail. I was going to delete it until Bobbie listened in."

She pressed play and the voice took over. In seconds, Jim's face turned the color of the fresh paint on the walls. Andrea looked at Bobbie and then back at Jim before halting the playback.

"What is it?" The tone of her voice reflected her concern.

"Let it play."

"But—"

"Play it," Jim insisted.

He listened for an instant longer before depositing the takeout on the desk. He rushed out of the office. Headed for the street. Didn't stop until he recognized the bar. He crossed the street and took up his customary seat.

He ordered a Crown Royal. Double. His drink of choice during the months he spent on the Baja. Those wasted months turned into a drinking binge when he gave up the search for the remains of the woman who eventually turned out not to be his wife.

"Son of a bitch, but it's never going to end." He said it to no one in particular as he played with the glass. Raised it to inhale the tart odor. Tilted and rolled the amber liquid in the glass until it ran thick down the insides. Imagined the taste.

"What was that?"

He turned to recognize the woman standing beside him.

"I knew you'd be here. I knew by the look on your face. What do you think you're doing, Jimbo?" Andrea placed her hands over his and sighed. She worked the glass out of his grip and pushed it away.

Jim stared into her blue eyes. Studied her face. Couldn't help smiling.

"Yes. I do, too. Now come on. Bobbie's waiting. She said she knew what the call was about. Why don't you tell me about it before we head back?"

Jim followed her to a two-top against a wall. She made him sit before going behind the bar. She returned with her version of a Virgin Mary and set it in front of him. The exact same drink was one she'd mixed for him that first time when he went searching for her in the bar, hung over and looking for sympathy.

He took a sip. "Thanks. I needed that."

They smiled at each other. Beneath the table, their knees touched. Neither pulled away. It was more than an hour before Andrea dragged him back to the office. She kept him sober, too.

"Thank goodness," Bobbie said. "What took so long? Where did you find him?"

"I mixed him a couple of drinks to keep him on the straight and narrow. But that wasn't the hard part. The hard part was listening to his story," Andrea admitted.

"He finally told you," Bobbie said.

"Yes. Some of it," Andrea admitted. "I think he left out a lot."

Jim regarded the women. Knew they cared about him if he knew anything. "You two realize that I'm not part of the furniture, right? I'm standing beside you." He eased down onto the expensive sofa and smiled. "This damned thing is worth more than I made as a cop up north. Play it again for me."

"Jimbo—"

"Play it. And what happened to the damned burritos? Do I have to do everything around here?"

Exasperated, the women answered, almost in unison. "We didn't want them to get cold. We ate them."

Bobbie took Andrea's arm and gently led her to the door. "Come on. We need to talk. Now."

The women went upstairs where Bobbie was letting Andrea stay until she found a place of her own. They were getting along. Telling stories about past likes and loves. Talking about Jim.

Bobbie could tell Andrea cared a lot for the man. Maybe she even loved him. If that was the case, a shared apartment was dangerous ground.

"I found a place of my own, Bobbie. I can move in another few days."

"What? Why? Don't you like it here?" Bobbie asked.

"You know why. You need your space. So do I. And you know I like you, too. But about Jim, we can't go on like this. I know how you feel about each other. It's obvious, even if you think you've been hiding it."

"I'm sorry—" She took the woman's hand.

"No need to be sorry. I knew what Jim was like before I fell in love with him. What almost happened in the everglades with the two of you will be the tip of the iceberg if we're not careful."

Andrea sat at the table. Bobbie put the coffee on. It was going to be a long morning. "I can't stay here above the office, Bobbie. It's, it's—"

Bobbie finished her sentence for her. "It's too tempting."

"Yes. He turned me down. I turned him down at first, just after I met him when I found out about you. But it's so difficult. Sometimes, when he looks at me—" Andrea said.

"I know. It was like that with me, too, at first. And it's been going on with me a lot longer than it has with you. I'll tell you about it sometime."

Bobbie turned off the stove and put the coffee pot on the counter. "We should go for lunch and talk."

"Lunch? We just had brunch," Andrea said.

"I know. But it's the laid-back, southern-girl thing to do, don't you think?"

Andrea checked the office on the way by. "He's gone. I have to go look for him. If he went back to the bar—"

"We'll go together. That voicemail got to him."

"And to think I almost deleted it because I thought it was some crank." Andrea said.

"Well, it might still be from a crank, in any case."

Andrea took a quick look in as they walked past the bar. "He's not there."

"That's a good thing, Bobbie told her. "Come on. Lunch or brunch or a good gab-fest, at the least, awaits."

2

I didn't want to alert the women. It was important I find out what was going on before putting them on edge or upsetting them.

Bobbie knew, of course. Or at least, she knew a little about it. Andrea was the one I didn't want to bring into it. But she was the one who listened to the message, and I was pretty sure the women would talk. That's what women do.

When I caught the pair of them in the very restaurant I was to meet up with the voice on the recording, I almost backed out. Their heads were bent over forks, picking at salads. Deep in conversation. Oblivious to everything going on around them.

When the women weren't chewing, lips competed to get words out. I smiled. Made it unobserved to a table in the back.

The man who sat down opposite me looked familiar. I couldn't put a name to the face, and he volunteered nothing to help me remember. It would come to me, eventually.

He pulled out an envelope. It crossed the table to

my side. In those brief seconds, a gunshot rang out. Old reflexes kicked in. I dived for the floor. My table mate grunted and toppled over on top of me. Two more shots and pandemonium erupted. Screams and a mad scramble of people and chairs and tables tipping took over.

I wiggled feet and hands to check for damages. I scrambled to roll out from beneath a body. My clothes were drenched in blood. Andrea and Bobbie caught sight of me as I struggled to stand. Screams accompanied yelling as the anxious pair dodged upended tables to make their way to me. Reeling from the attack, I got my arms around both and dragged them to the floor on hands and knees.

"Stay down. Stay down, dammit. I don't want to lose you. Either of you. I'll kick whose ever ass is left if I do."

I rummaged through the pockets of the man who took the bullet and dropped on top of me.

"What are you doing? Do you know him?" Bobbie asked.

There was nothing. I checked the table. The envelope was gone. I looked on the floor. It wasn't there. The son of a bitch of a shooter must have taken it. Which meant he knew what it contained.

"All right, you two. We need to get the hell out of here. The back way."

I grabbed hands and pulled them past swinging doors into the kitchen. I hauled ass past the grill and out the back door into a deserted alley. Strange how no one else made it out that way. We snaked our way via back alley and narrow pathways between buildings. Sirens and tires screeching on asphalt announced the arriving black and whites.

"Jimbo. Your clothes. Blood. You're bleeding. You have to get to a hospital," Andrea shouted. Her pale face stared back at me, looking like she was ready to pass out.

"You just noticed? I could have been dead by now and it would be your fault." I knew I went too far when silent tears streamed down her freckled face. I knew I went way too far when Bobbie socked me twice. Dammit but she could still swing a mean punch when she wanted to.

"Will you stop it? The woman is in love with you. Just how stupid are you? You have a major problem on your hands with your staff."

I looked at Bobbie incredulously. "What the hell are you talking about? And you're not my staff. We all work together."

She swung again, and I pulled back and spun her around and caught her in my arms. She drove a heel into my foot. I hung on and get her off the ground. She kicked, missed, and I set her down.

"Say that again."

"Andrea is in love with you. So am I. Deal with it. Now let's get back to the office. We have work to do, you dumbass."

Humbled, I allowed them to set the pace.

"And you better not try sneaking off to the bar," Bobbie said. "You're long past that. You have been for years. You don't drink, and all three of us know it. Well, except that one time with Andrea, but she helped you through that. How or why, I don't know. I don't want to know. If she's sleeping with you, I don't want to know. If you're sleeping with her, I don't want to know."

"Dammit, Bobbie. She's on your sofa in the living room every night. How can I be sleeping with her?"

"The office has a sofa. It's big enough. Anywhere is big enough."

At least she called it *our* office. "I am not sleeping with her." I couldn't deny I wanted to. Right from when she helped me into her bed. If I hadn't been so drunk—

Fortunately, she never asked.

"You will be. It's only a matter of time," she insisted. A woman who wouldn't take no for an answer. Imagine that.

"You're the one I love, Bobbie," I told her.

"And I see how she looks at you. I'm not jealous, but I should be. I know the effect you have on women. You had it on me, remember? You still do. Now get yourself in gear. I want to know who wants your ass hurting, disappeared, or dead. Besides Andrea and me, that is."

Shit. The last thing I wanted was for those two to know I loved both of them. It was bad enough when neither of them knew. Could it be worse than having someone hunt me down in order to kill me?

Heavy footsteps on the stairs announced at least two people on the way up. I listened to see if they'd stop, or go past to the third floor. I didn't get to wait. The office door opened and a uniform accompanied by someone I recognized—Detective Don Boyle—entered.

They looked the three of us up and down before

Boyle spoke. "Nash." Boyle looked around the office. "Nice digs."

"Surely. What can Dawson and Nash do for you?"

Detective Boyle held out a plastic bag containing a red envelope.

"Where did you get that? It looks like blood." As if I didn't know. How the hell did I miss it?

"You must be a detective," Boyle grinned. "It is blood. And why is your name on an envelope discovered under a body at my crime scene?"

That's why I missed it. I shrugged, not wanting to admit to anything. I took a pass on the detective's sarcasm, too. "I have no idea. Can I see it?"

There were bloody fingerprints visible beneath the clear plastic bag. Good ones, too. "Have you ID'd the prints yet?" I wondered if they might be mine, left behind in a hurry when I missed the envelope during the hurried search.

"No. We found it about an hour ago when we got the okay to move the body," Boyle admitted.

"So you haven't opened the envelope. Would you like me to do the honors?" It was worth a try.

"Good one. No. Not now. But after we have the prints checked, would you mind coming down to the station when we do open it?"

I couldn't say no to that. "Give me a call."

I handed out a shiny new card. In fact, I handed one to each of the officers. "If you know anyone—"

"We'll have them call you." The plain-clothes and the uniform departed.

"Jimbo, what the hell was that about? Were you supposed to get that envelope from the man who got shot?" Bobbie asked.

"Yes. It was already on the table. When the lead started flying, I forgot all about it. I got out from beneath the body with everything working. By then I couldn't find it. Then you pair of lumps showed up, and I wasn't hanging around with the two of you to drag out of the place."

"We'll have you know we are not lumps. In fact, we were just commenting at lunch on how nice our lumps appeared to be to you," Andrea said.

I flushed a bright red and headed for the door. "I know when I'm beat. I'm heading to this little bar I know. Who's coming?"

When I finally dragged their asses back to the office, the pair of them were shit-faced—lumps and all. I found myself leading two stumbling drunks up the stairs to Bobbie's. It wasn't all bad. I enjoyed having two women hanging onto me for support.

"You might as well stay, Jimbo. What else do you have to do?" Bobbie mumbled

"Not on your life. I'm headed back to the office. I know a nice comfortable sofa with room for me all by myself. I'll be back to cook breakfast. You have food, right?"

"I think it's obvious by now we're not living on your love."

I held up my hands. You can't say I didn't know when to surrender and beat a retreat.

3

Somehow, **I had managed** to get the wheezing John Doe onto the floor. The envelope he was so intent on handing over disappeared from sight. I had high-tailed it with the women, fearing the lead would keep flying. Would Boyle honor his word and call me before he opened said envelope? While the victim's voice on the recording sounded familiar, I had no clue if the man who left the voicemail was the same now dead man I met in the restaurant.

Another familiar voice interrupted my musing.

"Nash. I have something for you."

I must have missed the sound of the man's steps coming up the stairs. Detective Don Boyle poked his head around the open door before entering. His eyes roamed the office and halted at the bedding piled in disarray on the sofa.

"You on a budget or just sleeping on the job? Looks to me like you won't have to hire anyone to take messages."

I grinned, relieved it was the man who bugged me to apply for a P.I. license I never once considered. That he took the time to convince me and helped walk me through the paperwork impressed me.

"I need to replace those stairs with something that makes noise. What are you doing here? It can't be a social call at this hour. You have to be on the city's dime. My tax dollars at work—if I earned enough to pay taxes."

Boyle cracked a smile.

We had become friends after meeting on a case some time ago. He talked me into trying fishing, and although I had little time, what with trying to get the office organized, I found I enjoyed it. It reminded me of the times my grandfather had taken me fishing as a child.

"Is this about the body in the restaurant?"

"Sadly, no," Boyle said. "We still have nothing on him. I was in the area working a case and saw the lights on. I stopped by to drop off your partner's license."

"Bobbie's license? I didn't know she was ready. When did she take the test?"

"About a month ago. Her paperwork showed up. I was the one delegated to doing the background. Used to be a pilot, did she?" Boyle asked.

"As a matter of fact, yes. Still is, as far as I know."

Boyle's eyes wandered around the office, taking in the expensive furniture. "You're stepping up in the world. Nice. Fancy, too. You must be in the money."

"I wish. It's all financed. Credit cards." I held out my empty coffee cup. "All cash donations gratefully accepted. You want to go for steak and eggs?"

"Steak, you say? Business is that bad, is it?" Boyle held up his hands. "No time right now. Besides, if business is so bad, I'd have to pay courtesy of my city paycheck. I'll take a rain check. Did you say Bobbie? Roberta, right?"

"Yeah. That's it. Roberta. Or Bobbie. I think she prefers Bobbie."

"You don't know? I thought she was your partner."

"She is, but—"

Boyle appeared perplexed. "Women." He shook his head.

How could I disagree? "Yeah. Women."

Boyle waved and headed downstairs.

I wasn't sure why I couldn't admit to my relationship with Bobbie. It wouldn't have made any difference to the man. I chalked it up to my nervousness at starting a detective business that already had more listings and competition in the old yellow pages than anyone with a startup needed.

I settled in behind my desk and put my feet up. If I rolled the chair just right, it gave me a narrow view up the third-floor stairs to Bobbie's apartment door. Giggling and laughter drifted down. The two women in my life were getting shit-faced and probably talking about me again.

Before long, they'd be hung over and hurting. Tomorrow's breakfast wouldn't come soon enough. I couldn't wait to cast good-natured verbal abuse in their hung over direction. I turned my chair to look out the window at the neon stretching up and down the avenue. A soft knock and a blurred reflection appeared in the darkened window. Boyle? What was he doing back so soon?

"Jimbo—"

An even more familiar voice. "No. Go back to

bed. Breakfast is going to be a lot earlier than you want it to be. Now get."

"She's fast asleep," Andrea said.

I had to admit, the woman was tempting in the sheer nightgown that stopped high-thigh and all of a sudden. "Andrea, listen to me. I can't do it. Well, I can, but then I wouldn't be able to face Bobbie ever again. Besides, you're drunk and half naked and by the time I had breakfast on the table, you'd be embarrassed and feeling dirty."

"I wish," Andrea said.

"And just maybe I do, too. Now get the hell out of here before I spank you."

Andrea made the mistake of turning away while she was standing beside me. I smacked her ass way too hard. She retreated up the stairs on long, shapely legs, massaging her bright pink rear the entire way.

I didn't tell her about her bare butt hanging out like she was wearing a hospital gown. She probably knew it anyway.

I called into the office to give a situation report. For my trouble I was greeted by a recording.

There's no one in the office right now to take your call. We're at a gun range, practicing our aim in case our boss stops cooking us breakfast.

Women. My women. I reprogrammed the message before hanging up. Headed across the street to the bar. Ready to confront Nick. There was a minor problem with that. Was Nick the one I should be meeting?

I played dumb and took the first seat at the bar, purposefully ignoring anyone else. If Nicolas was the one, he'd have to approach me. At the same time, I couldn't be sure Nicolas wouldn't only be stopping to say hello and pass the time.

So who was Nicolas waiting for?

I needn't have wondered. Diana entered through the back door. My phone buzzed and I headed for the sidewalk in a hurry. With luck I got out fast enough that I wasn't recognized.

Bobbie's quick text forced me to rush to the office. I hurried up the stairs to confront the damage. What few files we had were scattered on the floor. The desk drawers were empty and on the floor. Sofa and chairs were tossed. Whoever it was made sure Andrea and Bobbie were away shooting guns and having fun.

"It could have been trouble if you two were here." Big trouble, by the look of it."

"If we had been, the break-in wouldn't have happened," Bobbie said.

"Maybe, but you don't know that. What I can't figure is why? We just moved in. There's nothing in our files that could possibly be of any value." We didn't even have any clients. Perhaps it was a scare tactic. But why? What was the message the caller left behind?

"This happened while I was on a stakeout," I told them.

"Who were you supposed to meet?" Bobbie asked.

I showed them the text and explained that while I was across the street from Andrea's bar, Nicolas junior showed up in his convertible. Diana showed moments later. "I have no idea if I was supposed to meet him, or someone else." I was flummoxed.

"We're a startup detective agency," I added. "We haven't even put our phone numbers out yet."

Andrea cast a worried glance in my direction. "Uhh, about that, boss—" She opened her laptop and brought up a web page. Our web page.

"What was your MIT degree in, Andrea?" I asked

"Well, my first was in computer science. And engineering. For starters."

"For starters?"

"Yeah. It's not important. I put the home page up a couple of days ago. It's not quite finished yet. That's why I didn't mention it. It's pretty basic. But it'll get a lot better, I promise."

It looked finished to me. Andrea was turning out to be a real asset. "So what you're saying is that anyone who was on the lookout could have found the page and paid us a visit?"

"Umm, not really. I didn't put the address up. Just the phone number. And email, of course. Oh, and look. We have an email already."

>>>you were outside the bar waiting that's why I didn't show myself i told you to wait inside

"Well, that answers that," I said. I was out of patience trying too hard to figure out who I was supposed to meet. I screwed up.

"You couldn't know, Jim. But maybe we should put up some cameras. Can you do that, Andrea?" Bobbie asked.

"If you've got the money, honey, I can do

anything. I put the server upstairs in your place in case someone noticed it down here and wanted to walk off with it."

"Do it," I told her. "We can afford it. How did you do at the gun range? Did you put any holes in Harry's roof?"

Bobbie appeared pleased with herself. "It was great. Your guy let us shoot a bunch of guns. He said we should take our time deciding before committing. He'll take trades, too, if we change our minds."

"Yeah, Jimbo. Uncle Harry is a great guy. He said we could go back a couple more times, and then decide. I'd like a nice dark blue one."

About that Uncle Harry thing, but I didn't say a word, what with Bobbie putting in her order.

"And I want badass in black," she said.

Now they were gun nuts. I shook my head and gazed at them in wonder. "By chance did Uncle Harry tell you not to point your guns at me, even if you want to pull the trigger?"

"No. But we convinced him to tell us all about you. You had a spell of going through the women, didn't you? No wonder you're gun-shy with Andrea."

Now I knew why the *Uncle* Harry. My face flushed. So did Andrea's.

"All right. Enough. I need to talk to your Uncle Harry about spreading unfounded rumors and innuendo."

Secretly, I was glad Harry told them the story. At least his version wasn't gossip.

"Now let's get this place cleaned up."

I dropped Bobbie's PI license courtesy of the state of Florida on the kitchen table. I dropped bacon in a frying pan and while I waited, I dropped six eggs into a stainless bowl, added a dollop of cream, and beat them into submission.

By then, it was time to bang on the bedroom door. The sleeping beauties crawled out to the waiting breakfast.

"So then, are you two a couple now?"

Bobbie's raised eyebrow gave me advance warning something was coming my way. "No, smartass. But then you should know already. Didn't you spend a night in Andrea's bed, too?"

I knew when to shut up. I banged dishes in the sink until the woman woke up for real. Bobbie didn't notice what was on the table in front of her until she sat down.

"Jim. Look. I got it. I got it. Andrea. Look." She held up the card. She stood up and did a pirouette while a huge smile lit her face. It was the biggest one in a while.

"So what's the big deal? You have a pilot's license, too. This is just one more to add to your hope chest." There was no way I could bring her down, even in fun.

"Yes, but this one is special. It means I get to work with you professionally. When can we go to the gun range? What's our first case together? Will we go on stakeouts, too?"

I was unprepared for the unbridled enthusiasm. While I accepted that we'd be working together, I never once considered she'd want to carry a gun.

"Well—" I hesitated. It gave Andrea a chance to

jump in.

"Jimbo, you can't arm her. If you think her punches are bad, you have no idea how her lead will feel when she ever slings it in your direction."

I took Andrea's sudden concern for my well-being with a grain of salt. "If you'd quit wandering down to the office half-naked in the dark, maybe she won't have an excuse to shoot either one of us."

"I wasn't half-naked. Didn't you notice?" Andrea asked.

I noticed. The woman had a body to go along with everything else I liked about her.

"What? Andrea? We had an agreement," Bobbie reminded her.

Oh-oh. Women violating agreements. Now that's never happened ever before. Maybe arming Bobbie wasn't such a smart thing to do after all.

"Don't blame Andrea. It was the booze talking. You two were so loaded I'm sure neither of you knew what the hell was going on. In any case, I sent her packing with a smack on the ass."

"So that's why you have that bruise. Andrea, you need to find a lover all your own. And Jim, I need to go pick out a handgun. You can come and help me."

Shit. Like a handgun and a man were even remotely similar. There was no way the woman would let me rest until I got her to Harry's.

"Yeah, Andrea. You want to join Bobbie at the range and pick one out too? You could shoot your own man and bring him home. Sort of like a catch and release program."

Then it occurred to me. "Did anyone remember to check the phone?"

Two hungover bodies scrambled to locate the office cell phone.

"There's a text. It's for you."

yesterday got screwed up big time. if you want more information you need to show up for a 2nd meeting

Bobbie looked perplexed. "Dead men don't send texts, Nash. Did you figure out who the man was? Did the police?"

"Boyle came by last night to drop off your license. He said they're working on it. And no, nothing about what was in the envelope. They probably want to get the prints back first."

"So what's next?" Bobbie asked.

I surveyed the mess of dishes in the sink. Maybe I'd be able to buy an hour of office alone time if I left them for someone else to do.

"My work here is done," I announced. "I'll see you both in the office."

The pair clattered down the stairs like teenagers headed to raid the fridge. "All right, you two. I'm off to see the wizard. Try not to shoot each other. Just in case, I love you both." I grinned on the way out the door and halted. "Tell your Uncle Harry I said hi, and that he shouldn't tell too many stories about me."

I fantasized about the two of them in a gun battle. I shook my head, wondered just how stupid I really was, and headed for the bar.

Except, I wasn't going drinking.

I wanted to scope exits, though I was familiar with the bar. It was where I met Andrea. I walked to the back anyway, opening restroom doors for a quick check. I pushed open the back door and stepped into the alley. I allowed the door to slam closed and walked both directions to see where the alley ended up.

Satisfied, I took the long way to the front and crossed the street. I waited, shaded from the unrelenting south Florida sun beneath an awning. I was hoping for a glimpse of what might crawl out of the swamp.

I recognized a car passing. It halted and backed into a parking spot. And there was the swamp creature. Nicolas junior. I snapped a couple of quick photos because I could, and Nick, looking fit and tanned and relaxed, strolled into the bar and out of sight.

Was it Nick who shot the man in the restaurant I was supposed to be meeting? Was he out to get me, and somehow missed? Had he found out about the vendetta I had against his father? Or did Diana perhaps have something to do with it?

There was only one way to find out.

4

It **didn't take three** of us long to bring the office up to what it was before the break-in. Something wasn't adding up, though. We had only a couple of open cases. Not so many opportunities to piss anyone off. Our file cabinets were virtually empty. The first drawer pulled would have told the thief that. So why was the office tossed?

"Is there any sign files were taken?"

Andrea looked at me and rolled her eyes. "Jim, we don't have any. Well, none that are still open that would cause this. Every old divorce case you did is finished long ago. Unless you've got something you're not telling us." She regarded me suspiciously. No rolling eyes this time. "Do you?" she asked.

"Everything I have is yours, so basically, no. I don't."

There had to be something else going on. I approached Andrea and placed my lips to her ear. If I ever needed a lesson in how attractive she was, that was it. I blushed, uncomfortable, yet needing to let her in on my suspicion.

"Jim? What are you doing?"

I inhaled her familiar perfumed scent. I noticed it before. I had slept in her bed, after all. My lips moved. I let warm breath tickle her lovely neck. Her face flushed.

"Do you know anyone who can sweep the place for bugs? I don't want to call in any favors unless I have to."

I knew disappointment when I saw it on a woman's face.

Andrea eased away from me. "Oh. So that's what that was about." Disappointed, she turned the tables with her own warm breath. "I can do it. MIT, remember? I know a place. I'll be back in a jiff."

I called up to Bobbie to help with the cleanup. I didn't get a chance to tell her about the bug. She danced around me and I was left with empty air.

"Are you trying to make up for last night, Detective Nash?"

I raised my voice, hoping she'd figure out what I was trying to do. "Make up for what? I told you nothing happened. Dammit, woman. How much more do you want from me?"

She didn't get it right off. Bobbie looked at me, aghast. Shock perhaps a better word. I motioned with my hand. Touched my lips. I covered my ears like a hear-no-evil monkey. Her eyes widened.

"You're a son of a bitch for doing it. And you better watch out. I might be your partner, but that doesn't mean I won't leave if you're not careful."

She got it and moved closer before lowering her voice. "So we're bugged. Convenient that we were all out of the office, wasn't it?" Bobbie lingered too close for too long. It was all right with me.

"You're right. Andrea is off picking up some equipment. For now, we have to act like we don't suspect a thing."

"So then, sex on the office desk is out of the question?" she whispered.

"Well, I wouldn't go that far."

Bobbie struggled to wriggle out of too-tight jeans. I might not be the smartest man in the world where it concerned women, but I knew better than to say anything about gaining weight.

"You're pregnant. When were you going to tell me?" I knew right off I shouldn't have said anything. She gave me a dirty look for my comment while hurrying to tug at my pants. We got done with the important parts on the office desk.

Before answering my question, she finished buttoning up. "I am not pregnant. I'm gaining weight."

I wasn't about to touch that with a fishing pole.

"And no wonder with you doing the cooking and me doing the eating. You're going to have to slow it down or I'll need a new wardrobe, Nash."

"Any excuse," I added.

She grinned back at me. "Pretty much."

Andrea balanced boxes and bags and fought to hold the building's door open while working her way past it. She struggled up the stairs, careful not to drop anything. She remained in the hallway and began quietly unpacking the black boxes and antennas to go with them. She inserted batteries and spread items on the surrounding floor.

"I'll be done in about twenty. Then you can come back."

She broke the office into quadrants and moved from one to the other, meticulous in her testing. Listening. Looking up and down. Shifting the devices as she swept the office corner to corner. She returned to the hallway to retrieve a second instrument and repeated her efforts.

Half an hour later Andrea waved us into the office. "All right, you two. The result of two naked half-moons on top of the shiny black desk are plainly visible."

Bobbie flushed. "She's going to make a good detective, don't you think, Jim?"

Caught red-handed and red-faced, looking out the window was the only practical thing to do.

"And, Mr. Detective, did you by any chance notice that she didn't call my ass fat?"

Jim regarded the women sheepishly. "Are you sure you're finished, Andrea? I could go back to the bar and wait."

"Not a chance." Andrea wrote feverishly on a sheet of paper before handing it over.

There looks to be four. Do you want to leave them in place? Would you like me to see if I can log onto them and do a trace? Do you want to remove them and try and determine which government agency is spying on us?

That last was a new one. Completely unexpected. Jim's face announced it as his voice lowered to a whisper. "Do you really think it could be feds?"

"I won't know until I get a look at the bugs. The one in the phone will be the easiest. The rest are part of the woodwork."

"What are you saying, Andrea?"

"Someone installed at least a couple of those things while we were having the place renovated."

"The government." It was a statement, not a question.

"Most likely."

Jim trusted the women implicitly. They had been with him when he tracked down Nicolas senior, the man responsible for his wife's murder. The three of them witnessed the old man tackled by an alligator and dragged into the swamp.

"Enough. Let's retire to the bar, ladies."

When my wife Pilar was killed in the aircraft accident, I completed my own investigation. I sent my report on her death to the FBI and Homeland Security. They did nothing to act on it. A wall of silence surrounded the aircraft accident once the government conclusions were reported in the newspapers. I was certain they branded me a crackpot. If that were true, why were they coming after me now?

We took a table at the back of the familiar bar while Andrea said her hellos to everyone and then brought us our drinks.

"Look, you two," I began. "I know you're proud of the office and everything you've done with it so far, but—" I hesitated before going on. All eyes were on me. "We have a decision to make."

"We know, Jim. It's going to be a pain in the ass until we figure it out. Is there any chance we can just fake it and carry on like nothing happened?" Bobbie asked.

Andrea threw in with Bobbie. "Yeah, Jimbo. Are we going to desert the office? Where else am I going to get to walk downstairs to find you sleeping on the office sofa?" Andrea rolled her eyes and the women high-fived.

"Dammit, you two. You want to be the death of me. If Bobbie doesn't want to shoot me for being unfaithful, you want to kill me with kindness."

Andrea looked at me, all wide-eyed and innocent. I wasn't convinced.

She said, "I don't think it's called kindness, but whatever. Call it what makes you happy."

I had enough. "Will you both stop it? We have more pressing matters to consider. The office is compromised. We don't know who's doing it. And we can't work out of the place until we find out."

It would be up to Andrea. "Woman, your instructions are to head back to the office. Try to find out what the hell is going on by any means possible or improbable and get back to us. Stat."

Andrea pushed off the barstool and saluted. "Si, capitán. With one detour."

She hurried out the door with Bobbie's eyes on her. It was plainly a look of admiration. "I think that woman is going to prove to be a real asset. Her background alone is worth a lot more than we're paying her."

"So then, does that mean you have no hard feelings about my sleeping in her bed?"

"Well, I won't say that, but then you never seemed to mind that I shared Nicolas junior's bed."

"What?" Until now, the subject never came up. In any case, I refused to consider it. With good reason.

"Tit for tat, so to speak. We're even. If it happens again, you're in deep doo-doo."

"Bobbie—"

She held up her hand. "I think we both know what we're capable of. I'll be faithful to you until you aren't any more."

"That's good enough for me. Will you marry me?" I reached into my pocket.

Bobbie regarded our surroundings, looking doubtful. She sighed. "In a bar? Really?"

Bobbie must have noticed the hurt look. Did the woman realize how serious I was? Maybe I was being more serious than she wanted. Maybe she wanted Andrea to come between us. It would let her off the hook by taking some of the pressure of the moment off of her.

Uncomfortable and embarrassed by my too-obvious mistake, I looked around the crowded bar, searching for Andrea. It was the only way I could think of to change the subject. "Where did she get to?" Then I remembered. I sent her on ahead.

"She mentioned something about a detour to find an art store before heading back to the office."

"Art store? I didn't know she was an artist."

Bobbie shrugged. "Me either. Let's get out of here. It's been a long day and I'm tired."

We returned to the office to discover Andrea had been busy with paint and brushes. She had a rough outline traced on canvas, and she was standing back, arms crossed, studying it.

"Oh. You're back. Good. I'll be here all night. I'll let you know when to come down, okay?"

I exchanged glances with Bobbie.

"Don't worry, you two," Andrea said. "I did what you asked."

I enjoyed getting up early to cook breakfast for the women in the cramped kitchen. The morning specialty was going to be my special grilled cheese sandwiches. The women liked them so much, they regressed to calling them *sammiches*. That was all right by me. It's what I ended up calling my grilled delights, too.

Andrea was usually the first to pop in to see how things were going in the kitchen. She claimed it was the fresh smell of coffee. Bobbie wouldn't be far behind, perhaps to ensure things stayed on the up-and-up. I enjoyed the good-natured banter they threw back-and-forth across the table as plates emptied and stomachs filled.

It was not to be this morning.

Andrea wasn't in the small apartment when I began breakfast prep—the one meal she never missed. She was probably still downstairs, working on her painting, and bunked out on the sofa. I sent Bobbie down to drag the woman away from her artwork.

I didn't think anything of the approaching sirens growing louder. We were on a main drag with plenty of nighttime action. I looked out a window over the street. Police cars and an ambulance were gathering below.

Bobbie came bounding up the stairs in a noisy crash of feet. Three steps at a time by the sound of it. Silence as she halted on the landing. Then a scream.

"Jim! It's Andrea!"

I rushed downstairs, still in my robe. I crashed into the office. At first glance, a colorful depiction the size of an old diner poster greeted me. The tape and paper were in the trash. Andrea's paints and brushes were neatly put away.

A second look saw Andrea laying crumpled on the floor. A look of wonder was frozen on her face. I halted. Shocked. Disbelieving what my eyes said to be true. I put my hands in both pockets of my robe. An old detective habit, one I never broke.

I bent over the woman. Checked her bruised neck with my eyes. My mouth moved. Barely. "She's been strangled. We better get Boyle on this."

The detective was already behind me.

"As soon as I heard the address, Nash," he said.

I stood up and turned. While I couldn't say I was happy to see him, given the circumstance, I was glad he was here. "Is that the way it looks to you?"

"No. That's the way it appears."

I moved off. Reluctant. Wanting to let Boyle do his job. Yet wanting to do it for him. He tilted the torso only enough to get a look. I used the same technique many times.

"Someone smashed in her head."

Boyle pointed to the pipe on the floor. In my haste I never noticed it. It was Andrea, after all. And I was busy silently cursing whoever it was did the deed. Cursing with a vengeance. Promising revenge.

"The pipe. You missed that. One end is covered in

blood. It's hard to see because it's so small. The blood is on the underside."

I finally noticed Bobbie. Back to the wall in the outer hall. Looking in. She too unbelieving.

"It's not right, Boyle."

Boyle grabbed my arm and dragged me into the hallway to join Bobbie. "You can't be here now. Neither of you."

"Dammit, Boyle. She worked with us. She's a friend and an amazing person."

I left out the part about maybe being in love with her. It wouldn't serve any purpose. Bobbie didn't need to know, even if she suspected.

"When we're done, Nash. For now, it's off limits. I'll put you both in jail if I have to. I can't have you contaminating the crime scene. You know that."

Boyle was right. I knew it. Bobbie knew it.

"Go back upstairs. Now, Nash," Boyle insisted. "Take her with you."

Yellow tape went up in the standard X to block the door to the office. There would be no access until the crime scene was cleared. Even then, the office would be sealed.

Not that any of it would stop us once Boyle and his crew disappeared.

5

I **struggled up the** stairs, heavy-footed, taking one at a time. My eyes unfocused. Outside the apartment, I paced the hallway aimlessly, mumbling to myself. Unable to go in. Cursing under my breath. Knowing Bobbie would be just as upset. Knowing I would be small comfort to her.

The door opened and she stepped in front of me. Blocked me. Forced me to halt in the narrow hall. I understood. She was waiting for me. Listening. She dragged me into the apartment and surrounded me in her arms.

"Jim—"

Numb. Unmoved. I stared coldly. Pushed her away, too engrossed in my own sense of loss to recognize hers. "Not this time."

A single tear rolled down Bobbie's cheek. "Dammit, Jim. Keep it together. I'm just as upset. You need to settle down if we're going to find out who did this to Andrea."

I ignored her and kept up the pacing, back and forth. I ended up in the bedroom where I finally dressed. I opened the door and stepped out of the small apartment into the hallway. Bobbie slapped me and dragged me back into her apartment.

The slap was a good one. I stared, open-mouthed. Raised a hand to my cheek and rubbed. "I can't stay here. I'll sleep in the office tonight."

"You don't know that the person who murdered Andrea wasn't looking for you. Or for me."

"I have a gun, dammit, and I'm capable of using it."

"Not if you're fast asleep. We don't know if the murderer has a key. There's no way for us to even know if the office was locked."

"I've got to do something. I'm going down to see Boyle."

The detective refused entry. "You know the rules, Nash."

Boyle escorted me downstairs. He led me to a black and white and opened the door. The black and white's interior was lit by a flash of light. I was pretty sure it captured a look of surprise, as though I was the guilty party. The morning's headline would no doubt be flashed across the city's papers and web sites.

ALLEGED ACCUSED IN WOMAN'S MURDER

At least I wasn't still in my bathrobe.

Boyle slammed the door. I ended up trapped in the back. The media feeding frenzy went on and on, no doubt fed by my ignoring them. An hour later, Boyle tapped on the window and opened the door. The sun was rising to announce another day of endless blue sky and sunshine.

And death. Andrea's death.

"That girl was a pretty talented artist," Boyle said. "I can tell by what she did with the painting. It's a fascinating abstract of a Miami street scene painted in full color."

Maybe Boyle was being a little too artsy for my liking, but his comment edged out some of my despair. I didn't go near the office. I climbed straight to the third floor and began tossing the remnants of breakfast in the garbage.

"Bobbie, I'm heading out. I'll see you tonight, okay?"

"Where are you off to?"

"I have no idea. I need to get away from here."

"Are you coming back?"

If I hesitated she'd be on me like a dog worrying a bone. "Of course I'll be back."

I pursed my lips and walked out of the apartment. I felt the weight of the world on my shoulders. Would I be up to the task? Would I be able to find Andrea's murderer? I had to get away. I needed to know what I knew, what I didn't, and how I'd find out the rest.

Who I loved. Who I didn't love.

And then Bobbie called out the door, reminding me who I loved.

"I'll be waiting for you."

Who she loved.

Bobbie waited as long as she could. By mid-afternoon, she became impatient and began cruising the bars, on the lookout. Drinking was the last thing she needed Jim to be doing. In his present condition and suffering the loss of Andrea, there was no telling what he'd be capable of.

By early evening, she was in panic mode. There was no sign of the man anywhere. If he was bar-hopping, it wasn't in their neighborhood. She returned to the apartment and tried to calm her fears by thinking back to how they met. That lasted for about five minutes.

She walked down to the office, still concerned. Still worried. She discovered Jim behind his desk. It was the last place she thought of looking. He was staring up at the mural Andrea painted. In the familiar street scene, two women stood arm in arm in the window beside the neon sign. They looked down at a man in the street. He was happily waving and looking up at them.

"For the first time in a long time, I don't know what I'm doing any more, Bobbie. I want to run away."

"Just what Andrea would want you to do. I think I'll join you. Maybe we could go to an all-inclusive and forget everything."

Jim stared at her, cold and unfeeling.

She went on. "Suck it up and get your ass upstairs. It's past bedtime for both of us. If you still feel that way in the morning, I'll help you tie your shoes. Hell, I'll even pack your bag and start the car for you."

Cheerful whistling woke Bobbie. So did banging pans and clinking silverware. The accompanying smell of bacon and eggs and toast did its job to revive her. She threw on a robe and went to investigate.

"Burnt toast. My favorite. Andrea's too, remember?"

He returned her smile. "The only reason you two like burnt toast is because it informed you both I was out here making breakfast the instant you smelled it. You two are incorrigible." He hesitated and corrected himself. "Were incorrigible. Shit. Now sit and eat like you enjoy it without her."

She took her place across the table.

"You need to get to the gun range today. Right after it opens. I can't let you leave that place until you've picked out a weapon. The approval should have gone through by now."

"I already have one," Bobbie told him.

"You do?" That was news.

"Yeah. Andrea picked out a dark blue .357 automatic. I'll do the paper to transfer it to my name."

"Dark blue? What's with that?"

"She said it set her blue eyes off perfectly."

Jim smiled and shook his head, reminded of Andrea. As if he needed to be. Women. Always thinking of color-coordinating. "Let me have a look."

Bobbie retrieved the weapon from the night table in the bedroom. She removed the loaded magazine and racked the slide. She handed it to Jim, assured that it was safe to do so.

"You're learning. Good." He smiled. Andrea made a good choice. Reliable. Sized right. It fit Bobbie's hand perfectly, too. He'd make sure she kept it. That she wore it. All the time.

"Aren't you the cheerful one this morning. It's about time. I was starting to worry after last night."

He handed the weapon back to her. "We need to find a place to live. We can rent this place out. Maybe another bartender or a waitress. We can afford not to charge much for it."

"I agree," Bobbie said. "Now what's the plan to avenge Andrea?"

He looked at her, surprised at the way she so swiftly slipped from joy to revenge. "Officially, I'm going to let Boyle see this one through. Neither one of us can keep the distance this would require."

The look on Bobbie's face told him she agreed. "And unofficially?" she asked.

"I thought maybe Nicolas junior and Diana might know something. Last I saw them, they were meeting at Andrea's former bar in the middle of the afternoon."

"Then start there. I'll go to the office and poke around. Maybe Boyle missed something," Bobbie said.

"Good idea. Try not to disturb anything. I'll be back later to help."

She was about to wisecrack at his *disturb* comment, but thought better. They were both despondent and exhausted. "If I'm not home, I'll be at the range. I want to try on this sexy blue model before making it my own."

I walked to the bar where Andrea worked before I hired her away. The man behind the counter expressed dismay and shock at the news. I let him look at one of the photos I had of Nicolas entering the bar. It was blurry. His face was turned away.

"Yeah. I think he comes in here. It's hard to tell from that picture. He's not a regular, but often enough. Sometimes a woman comes in through the back door to check up on him. Don't ask me more than that. I have no idea."

"Describe the woman for me."

The bartender took a moment. "Tall. Long legs. Great tits from what I could tell. She never came all the way in. She stayed by the doorway, like she was spying. Or maybe waiting on someone else before she came in."

Diana. What was she doing spying on Nicolas? Last I saw her, Nick was between the woman's legs and they were having a great time.

"Did this one ever meet up with anyone?" I pulled up a photo on my phone and held it out. The bartender titled his head at the photo of Nicolas. It was more in focus.

"Not that I remember. He just came in, sat down, and usually it was Andrea that served him. Wait, is that the same guy as in the other picture?"

Andrea? Waiting on Nicolas? Or waiting for Nicolas? Hair stood up on the back of my neck. Something wasn't right. And she definitely never mentioned it to me.

Did Bobbie know?

Next stop was the upscale bar where Diana worked. I knew better than to ask when she came on shift. Instead, I took a quick look for a woman with long legs and a nice rear in a tight skirt. Disappointed, I left and made for home.

I arrived at the office where Bobbie was wrapping up her look around the place, searching for something, anything, that Boyle might have missed.

"Well?"

Perplexed, she shook her head and avoided my gaze by staring out the window. "I tried. I looked at everything. Every piece of paper and notepad and phone message and incoming call. Nada. Nothing." She rubbed at her eyes.

I took her in my arms. "It's all right. We'll figure it out. Did Andrea ever mention that she was seeing Nicolas?" I tried to be nonchalant about the loaded question. It didn't work. Bobbie almost jumped out of her skin.

"What? Seeing Nicolas? No way."

"Not even after I turned down her advances?" I asked.

"Not even then, Jim. She told me about it. I understood. She was attracted to you from the moment she met you. Why else would she invite you up to her apartment and let you sleep in her bed?"

"Yeah, but—"

"Woman scorned? Not Andrea. No way. You saw how Nicolas junior was with Diana, even when that woman was sleeping with Nick senior. Andrea thought he was a pig. I know, because she told me so."

Who was I to doubt? Except.

"Well, there was something going on," I said. "Nicolas was meeting her in the bar. I confirmed it with the bartender today. And Diana has something to do with it, too. She was keeping an eye on Nicolas."

Was she keeping an eye on Nick and Andrea?

"Maybe Diana was jealous. Maybe Nick was having meetings with other people in the bar. He recognized Andrea. Perhaps he was trying to convince her to go out with him," Bobbie said.

"Could it have been some rando that killed her? Someone who saw us moving in. Doing renovations. Waiting for the right time to approach her. A customer from the bar where she worked, maybe?"

"That leads us back to Nicolas. And Diana. Let's start there."

There was something else.

"The building maintenance guy came by to see if we needed help straightening up the office," Bobbie said. "He wanted to talk to you about something, too."

Andrea's parents were elderly and unable to travel. It fell on Bobbie and me to handle the details of Andrea's trip home to her grieving family and her final resting place. We drove north to the small town to deliver the cremated remains of our good friend.

By then, Detective Boyle had been in touch with them. It provided a measure of comfort that I was able to reassure the family Boyle was a competent police officer. That he'd give Andrea due diligence. That he wouldn't rest until he solved her murder.

We remained for the duration. Andrea was keeping her parents up to date about her new job. About both of us. About how she was finally happy to be using her skills to help us. Bobbie ended up in tears, and I wasn't far off when Andrea's mom and dad told us this over their kitchen table.

When it was over, I promised the family we would do what we could to keep them informed from our end. I wasn't hopeful, but I did what I could to reassure them.

The drive back to the city was long and silent. We ended up arguing about how we'd solve Andrea's murder. I wasn't concerned, since I knew Boyle to be more than capable.

"How, Bobbie? What could we do?"

"We should have promised," she said.

"Andrea once said that promises were hard for her to keep. I believed her then, and I still do now. We'll do what we can. We have suspects."

I wasn't entirely convinced. On one hand, Nick and Diana were our ideal suspects. I didn't know why, yet. On the other hand, if they weren't—

"Bobbie, we need to find out if you're next on the list of dead women," I told her. She wasn't happy to hear it.

"You want me to start hanging out in bars? I did that a lot in Alaska."

"Yeah, I think we already know how that went. Remember how those old guys in the hospital were so friendly and so anxious to see you every day?"

"It was only because my gown was wide open in the back. You liked seeing my ass too, remember?" she reminded me.

"I like it a lot more now that it's not black and blue. We need a plan."

Bobbie shook her head. "I remember how your plans go, too. I'll be sure to get out the Kevlar."

Finally Bobbie agreed we should pursue the

Nicolas-Diana link, if there was one. We agreed to split it down the middle. Bobbie drew Diana. In fact, she insisted on it.

"I don't want you checking out that woman's legs long enough to lose track of what you're supposed to be doing," she said with a grim look.

I gave her a look that said *I'm a professional*. She wasn't having any of it. She jabbed me in the shoulder for good measure. I held up my hands.

"Just remember, Nash. If you surrender to anyone, it better be me. Tonight. When you get home."

I couldn't argue that.

If Nicolas and Diana were involved in something shady, there wasn't any way I'd be able to become involved. Bobbie, on the other hand, well, she'd already been a party to Nick junior's pool parties. Maybe she'd be capable of convincing Nick she wanted back in.

If that was the case, Diana would be blowing steam out of both nostrils and pawing at the ground if she thought Bobbie might come between her and Nick. I hoped I wasn't wrong.

Why else would a woman be checking up on her lover in a seedy bar on the sunny side of the street?

There was something else. Diana's comment about a boat blowing up. It slipped out when she was tending to my wounds, courtesy of Bobbie's friends in Diamondhead and the sloop she crewed.

It could have been a joke on her part. If it was, how could she possibly know anything about it?

How would she know I once sailed on a sloop that exploded before my very eyes?

Something wasn't adding up. I just didn't know what.

I checked my watch. We still had a few hours. If we could locate Nicolas, we'd get a head start on tomorrow.

The convertible wasn't at Nick's place. I doubled back and cruised parking lots at the more popular downtown hot spots, but I couldn't get a line on it. I wasn't certain where Diana lived, so that was out for now. I sent Bobbie a text.

did you get anywhere with Diana? where does she live? and is Nick's car at her place? i can't seem to locate him

When she finally got back to me, I wasn't happy.

i'm talking to him now he's even more good looking than I remembered

I knew better than to say a word. It was starting to look like I'd be the one alone in the apartment tonight. I stopped at the office. My intent was to search an online 411 directory, until I realized I didn't know Diana's last name.

I needed to do something about that.

6

I stayed up well past midnight, waiting. Checking the phone. Pretending to be busy until Bobbie showed. She never showed and I gave up, finally. It wasn't like her not to text. I climbed the stairs and slept fitfully at Bobbie's place. Every noise woke me, expecting to hear the woman's steps on the stairs.

Thoughts of Andrea intruded. The soft scent of her perfume lingered in the bedroom beyond the sheets Bobbie laundered. I couldn't help dwelling on the reality that although I left the police department, women I cared for were still getting killed on my watch.

At 4 a.m. I got out of bed for good, dressed, and wandered down to the office. I flipped on the single light on the desk and aimed it at the mural. I stared at Andrea's finished work hanging on the wall. It only made it even more evident that she cared for us. As we cared for her.

I wasn't able to keep her alive. Where did that fit into the caring equation?

I put my feet up on the desk, leaned back in the chair, and just about dozed off when I heard a groan.

Bobbie rolled over on the sofa. Long hair shifted and covered her face.

"What the hell? What are you doing down here?" My feet slipped off the desk and banged onto the floor. She blew a puff of air. It floated her hair away and she could see.

"I didn't want to disturb you."

The odor of stale cigarette smoke wafted through the room. There might have been more than a whiff of beer, too. "Where have you been? Don't lie. I can smell it all over you."

Bobbie rolled into a sitting position and planted dirty bare feet firmly on the floor. "Very good, detective."

What the hell had that woman been up to? "Your feet are black as tar. What happened to your shoes?"

She leaned over and looked down at the floor. Pulled at her blouse and sniffed. "Ugh. Cigarettes." She went back to looking at her feet. She wiggled her toes. "Well, they still work, at least. What's new with you, Jimbo?"

I raised an eyebrow at the woman's expression. Since Andrea died, she'd taken to using it. I didn't mind. I liked being reminded. "Not so much. I was upstairs, waiting for you. I got restless sleeping in an empty bed, so here I am."

Bobbie raised her feet off the floor and went back to stretching out on the sofa. I think she knew it was Andrea I missed.

"You must have danced up quite a storm last night in the smoke-filled biker bar."

She yawned. "You'd make a good detective, detective."

"Thanks. I think. Now then, what gives?" I asked.

"I ran into Nicolas yesterday. He took me on a tour. Can I have a cup of coffee? And maybe throw a burrito in there just for old time's sake. Please?"

Jim departed and Bobbie hastily tossed a burn phone into the desk and closed the drawer. She made a single phone call from the office phone before scurrying up the stairs.

She ran through the shower. Scrubbed at her filthy feet. Dressed. Found a pair of sneakers. Brushed her hair. She threw an old backpack on the bed and searched through the dresser. She tossed all manner of shorts and underwear and bikinis into the bag. Went through the closet for skirts and blouses.

Bobbie forced the zipper closed on the bulging bag and threw it over a shoulder. She hurried down the flight of stairs to the second-floor landing. Hesitated to step lightly past the office. Then down the final flight. She exited the building into the early morning sunlight just beginning to kiss the tallest buildings.

She hurried down the street in the opposite direction to that of the burrito shack where she knew Jim would be headed and made for a waiting car. The driver reached across to open the door and smiled. "All ready?"

Bobbie nodded wordlessly and slipped past the open door to slide across the bench seat beside the driver.

"You're looking pretty good after last night," the driver said.

He busied himself powering down the convertible's top. "Thanks. So are you. Now let's get going before he comes back."

Bobbie leaned against him. Kicked off her runners. Put her feet up on the door. She wiggled her bare toes and allowed the cool breeze to blow away all of her cares and concerns but the one sitting next to her. The man's arm went around her.

He was eager to talk. "It's about time you dumped that loser."

Bobbie settled back to listen.

"I have to admit, I never thought you'd do it."

She didn't answer. She waited, wanting to know what would be next.

"Things are going to be getting a lot better for you. You'll see. That walk-up you were shacked up in is nothing compared to what I'm going to do for you, baby."

Bobbie smiled outwardly. Inwardly, she seethed. It was the same tired, old line she'd been hearing for years before she met Jim. This time, she was going to make sure she put her own spin on it to avenge the death of her friend.

No matter what it took.

It was too early for burritos. Instead, I managed to corral a batch of warm croissants from out the back door of a local bakery. I climbed the stairs to the second-floor office, whistling all the way.

I was looking forward to hearing Bobbie's story about last night's hangover that was so bad she had to sleep on the office sofa. I'd wait her out, knowing eventually the story about the missing shoes and the dirty feet would come out. The croissants would help get her jaws moving.

"Breakfast is served, miss. No sunglasses this time, I'm afraid."

Nothing. She wasn't in the office. I put the bag down and walked up to the apartment. The bedroom was a mess, as though someone searched it.

I checked the closet. Bobbie's well-worn backpack, the one she carried the first time we met, was gone. I looked around for a note. I even checked the fridge for reminders of forgotten tasks.

It was as though she disappeared. Or gone on the run. Was she running from me? Something else? If she was running, who was she running with? Or to?

I shrugged and went down to get the croissants. I cooked up bacon and eggs and had a thoroughly enjoyable breakfast—but for the missing Bobbie. I finished and stood to look out the window overlooking the street. The sun was up. The buildings on the west side were coming out of shadow. It would be another gorgeous day.

I sipped coffee and contemplated life while regarding the quiet street scene and life in general. Andrea murdered. Bobbie gone. The business I thought they wanted to share was all over before it even started.

I went back to the office and fired up my laptop. I typed briefly and then sent the page to the printer, waiting for it to spit out. I went back to my desk, sighing as I contemplated the single page.

I was in the shit now. I thought back to Diana's statement in Diamondhead, the one about not blowing up the yacht. I still couldn't figure it. How in hell had she known anything about that? I was certain I never mentioned it. Why would I? She was merely a pair of sweet-looking long legs and big breasts during a weak moment in my life.

In my mind I set her aside, only to have her come roaring back. The yacht. The explosion. Her words. What was it she said? I searched memories of that day.

I no sooner got my feet up on the desk than they slipped and slammed to the floor. It came back to me, like a bolt out of the blue.

Don't blow this one up, too.

That was it. *Don't blow this one up.* I had it. And then, the word, *too.* As though there had been another one. But how did she know? How could she? I didn't know her from Adam—or even Eve. I'd never seen Diana before in my life. Our paths never crossed before that day in the Diamondhead yacht club.

I was exhausted enough to try and get some sleep, finally. All of this thinking and Andrea's murder and Bobbie's disappearance and trying to remember had run its course. I trudged up the stairs, undressed, and collapsed into bed.

It was only half-past morning.

The ringing phone brought me back to consciousness, interrupting the dream about Kara and Bobbie and Andrea and so many others forcing their way into my subconscious. I was happy to be disturbed.

I jumped out of bed, too groggy and late to take the call. I checked the phone. No message. I shrugged and stumbled back to bed. Tossed and turned remembering the dream. Unable to sleep, I showered and dressed to face what was left of the day.

I checked both apartments. Bobbie hadn't returned. I looked for Andrea's handgun. It, too, was gone. Both disappeared. She must have packed everything up and left after dispatching me for the food.

Oh well. I got along just fine before Bobbie came into my life. I'd get along without her. It was then I realized I was beginning to miss her already. Why else would I be thinking about her?

It was Friday night. Still early. I locked the office door, walked down the stairs, and headed out into the busy street. Cars honked. Passengers yelled. Music blared from the clubs, a siren call for the drinkers and the boozers and the small-time druggies. Neon blazed and blinked and buzzed against the background of buildings and dark sky.

Andrea's former bar presented itself, relatively speaking a bastion of quiet and sensibility compared to the neon and loud music I put behind me. I hesitated, wanting to. Not wanting to. I walked on by, halted briefly at the bar where I picked up Diana's trail after she left Diamondhead, and entered. I spotted her from the doorway, turned tail in a hurry, and exited onto the sidewalk.

I needed to pick an exit. The smokers would be at the back in the alley, grabbing a quick one before going back in. Diana didn't smoke. She'd probably avoid that crowd, not wanting to encourage a stray male to follow her home. I took a chance and settled in at the sidewalk café across the street and ordered coffee.

It was a good location. The street was narrow. Only two lanes of traffic to obscure the view of the bar. I found out her apartment was up the same street. If she would head there after work. I'd have gone there, and waited. But I needed to know more about her before doing that.

It was still eating at me. That comment. *Blow it up. Too.* The yacht I shared with the love of my life. At least, Kara had been the love of my life back then. Now, I understood different.

After our assignment was over, we sailed through the Canal in Saskia's sloop and headed north up the west coast. Got married in an ancient Spanish mission. The intent being to hole up off at an Ensenada marina and take a few days to relax and enjoy the sights and sounds of Mexico.

It hadn't happened. I took the dinghy ashore in a search for a berth in the harbor. I was forced to offer a *mordida*—a bribe—to get one. On the way, I picked up some of our favorite takeout and headed back in the dinghy.

That's when it happened. In front of my eyes. The yacht—Saskia's yacht—exploded. I spent months searching. Found nothing. I retired to Mexican cantinas and beer and tequila and eventually sobered up enough to cross the border and head home.

It was all for nothing.

Now I was on the watch for a woman I didn't know who brought it all back with one short, six-word sentence. Did she even know what she was saying?

Don't blow this one up, too.

I was rewarded when Diana strode purposefully out of the bar. Her shoulder bag swayed at her side. Each swing matched the sultry arc of her hips. She stopped briefly. Her head turned from side to side. Checking the nighttime reflections in a shop window, no doubt.

My senses went on alert. She was looking for a tail. What the hell? No one does that. Well, all right, no one but someone who needs to know.

Was she off on a romantic rendezvous? Buying drugs? Selling them? Had she spotted me across the street guzzling coffee and trying not to go to the restroom?

I kept after her, strolling behind, hands in pockets as though doing the tourist thing. She turned onto a side street. It was darker, and the crowd thinned immediately. It was going to be difficult to follow her and remain unnoticed.

With no crowds to hinder her progress, her pace increased. She stopped less. Looked over her shoulder not at all. She had to have convinced herself no one was following.

Almost running now, she crossed the street, cut through another alley, and came out in front of a three-story building. She halted, looked around, and then punched in a code. The door clicked. Her hand hesitated. Her head turned to check the street. When she didn't see anyone, she pulled open the door and disappeared.

No address. There was nothing. No number. No sign. No window markings. I checked across the street to get a number. Should I stay and wait, or head back to the office and do some research?

7

There wasn't much I could do about finding office help, given my lack of enthusiasm. I went so far as to return to Andrea's former bar to inquire if there was someone who might want to answer phones and sit in on interviews to take notes.

Not surprisingly, no one volunteered for even a part-time shift. It seems they all heard what happened to Andrea. Disappointed and dejected, I headed home through noisier, drunker crowds and music louder in the night.

The *Help Wanted* sign in the window was missing again. I cursed the neighborhood and stopped to pet a big black Labrador sitting outside my building's door. The dog seemed friendly enough. He swept the sidewalk with his tail while he looked up at me with warm brown eyes. So maybe I owned the crappy attitude after all. Instantly cheered up, I left the dog behind and climbed the stairs, intending to return with a bowl of water.

The woman was waiting on the top step. Disheveled short hair. Head bent and buried in a phone. Blue light illuminating her face. Fingers traced patterns back and forth, tapping rapidly. Typical behavior for people her age, from what I could tell.

She realized someone was watching. Looked up and then back down at the phone. Her other hand fished in her bag and ended up handing over my sign. "You this guy?" she asked.

So that's where it went. "Yes, I'm that guy. Come in."

I unlocked the office, turned on the lights, and motioned for the woman to take a seat. She sat down before placing a laptop bag and an oversize shoulder bag beside her on the sofa. The phone disappeared.

So maybe she wouldn't be checking texts while she did the interview. Impressive. Her appearance wasn't. Clothes wrinkled. Clean, though. She didn't smell. Bedhead. I wondered if she had a hairbrush in the oversize bag. Perhaps she needed the job. I rapid-fired questions, one after the other.

"Can you type?"

Her mouth opened to answer.

"Can you take messages?"

She didn't get a chance.

"Do you mind drinking coffee? How do you feel about burritos? Ever been on the internet? Do you know how to use a broom? Can you take shorthand?"

That last was a joke. Maybe the one about the broom, too. She looked at me like I was nuts. Her eyes almost rolled. She must have thought better and closed them instead. Her eyelids fluttered.

"Of course I can take shorthand. And it's yes to all the other questions, too, by the way."

I held out my hand. "I'm the Nash part of the neon sign hanging in the window. Jim. Pleased to meet you— uhh, what's your name again?"

She looked at the sign and back at me. "Matilda. My friends call me Maddie. Maybe when I get to know you, you could call me Maddie, too."

I slid the application tentatively across my desk, thinking if I changed my mind, it would be too late by the time her hand closed on it.

She stood up and a tall, lanky girl with short-cropped blonde hair bent over the form. She took her time with three or four of the questions. Straightened. Read and reread. Thought before using the pencil. Not once did she use the eraser.

Maybe she was thoughtful. Or she wanted a job. Any job. Bad.

"So where did you learn shorthand? I don't know a single person who even knows what it is these days."

She didn't look up from the form. Kept writing. Maybe she was a multi-tasker. Maybe not.

"It was a hobby of mine back in high school when I got bored. It confused the hell out of everyone. The boys asked to borrow my notes and then it got out that they couldn't read them. No one ever asked again.

Well hell. A thinking man's woman for sure.

"You married?"

It wasn't a question on the form. It wasn't even a question that should be asked.

"Nah. I'm not stupid."

"Ever worked behind a bar?"

She nodded, but it didn't appear to be an enthusiastic nod. She went back to the form and ran a line through something.

"Kids?"

She shook her head and I got that look again. If Bobbie was around, she'd approve of the woman's attitude, for sure. Andrea, too.

"You heard about my last office person?"

She reached into her bag and fished for a bit before pulling out a knife. She placed it on the sofa. She went back in with both hands. Fumbled in the bottom of the bag. Muttered. Pulled out a nice S&W hammerless. Five-shot. I noted she gripped it by the frame. She aimed the grip at me and flipped open the cylinder before offering it to me.

I shook my head. "Nine-millimeter?"

She nodded. "Uh-huh."

At least she wasn't chewing gum. "All right then. You're hired. But first I need to see the paper."

She emptied the bag onto the sofa and rummaged through the mess. Cursed quietly. Came up with the permit and held it out.

Let it be current, please, I said to no one in particular.

"Perdido. The Redneck Riviera." It came out before I even thought about it. Spanish for lost. The woman just might be living out of her car after all. So maybe she was lost, too. Nothing wrong with that.

"Yeah. On the panhandle by the border with Alabama." She began putting everything back into her handbag. It took a while.

I took my time examining the permit, because I could. The carry permit's expiry wasn't far off. I made sure my lips weren't moving. She probably thought I was a slow reader.

"Looks good. Now show me the handgun again."

Her hands went back into the bag. There was a loud snap. My ears perked up, sort of like the dog downstairs when I paid him some attention. I straightened in my chair. Tensed involuntarily.

She pulled a zipper, and I couldn't fathom the reasoning behind a handgun on the bottom of a purse. It would be a magnet for all kinds of dust and dirt and anything else that might be at the bottom of a woman's shoulder bag. That, and never be in a hurry to use it. Maybe that's why.

She hauled it out, grip first. Flipped the cylinder. Ejected a moon clip with five rounds into her hand. I didn't make a move to take it.

"You got a holster?"

Matilda shook her head while replacing the lead. I opened a couple of drawers before reaching into one. I handed over a well-used brown clip-on.

She made to reach. Hesitated.

"It's all right. You can use it until you decide you want to quit and move on."

Like the rest of them. I didn't say that out loud.

She smiled and stood up and holstered the S&W before tucking it into the back of her belt. Inside her jeans. She pulled out her shirt to cover it. "It's a good fit. Thanks. When do you want me to start?"

The phone on the desk in front of her rang. She answered it like a pro. "It's for you, Mr. Nash."

I took it and put a hand over the speaker. "Jim. My name is Jim. Or you can call me Nash. That's okay, too. And if you want to work part-time for some spare cash, there's a job opening in a bar down the street."

She frowned, shook her head, and then broke into a huge-ass grin. She must have realized she had the job. "You can call me Matilda."

My own head shook like a bobble-head doll stuck to a dashboard. Another smartass. It seemed like my life was doomed to find every single one on the face of the earth and hire them all. I shifted into work mode and spoke into the phone.

"Yeah. What can I do for you?"

Matilda disappeared without a word. Maybe she thought I didn't have a sense of humor. I was still listening when she showed up with the black Labrador. She sat down at the desk that used to be Bobbie's and the dog plopped down beside her, ears perked, looking proud. Maybe he was happy she finally had a job. The food would no doubt be better. There'd probably be more of it, too.

The dog's tail mopped the floor. Not a problem as far as I was concerned. He looked at me and seemed to smile, like he had nothing better to do. I smiled back. I didn't have anything better to do, either.

The call ended and I left the office to go upstairs. I dug around beneath the sink and came up with an old stainless-steel bowl. Filled it with water from the tap and some ice cubes. Took it downstairs. The dog refused to drink until Matilda gave him the okay. Then he looked up at me, down at the water, and dove in.

"Good boy, Friday," she said, and slapped Friday's side. The tail-wagging turned serious. Her other hand busied itself pulling open drawers and coming up with note pads and message forms and pens and pencils. Eventually, the top of the desk turned into something that looked like it belonged in an office.

Too bad Bobbie wasn't around to take notes.

Friday finished splashing and settled into the empty space between desks again. Against the wall. Looking like he'd be keeping an eye on things until everyone got the lay of the land.

"Nice dog." He ignored me. Matilda didn't.

"Yeah. I think so too."

"So what's a woman from the far reaches of the panhandle doing in Magic City?"

She squirmed and looked down at Friday and then back up at me. Like her dog did before diving into the water. "Do I get the job?"

"You aced it. Best interview ever."

She looked doubtful. "I was the only one, wasn't I?"

She had me there. "I only put the sign out this morning. These things take time."

"Uh-huh."

I found a set of keys for the doors and handed them over. They disappeared into Matilda's handbag to share space with the handgun in its holster when she wasn't wearing it. The knife, too.

With everything in the office under control, I could use the opportunity to do a bit of actual detective work. *Detectiving*, Andrea had called it and laughed. It was time to connect with Diana. Try to learn what the woman was up to.

"I'm going to be out of the office for a bit doing some detectiving." I grinned a big-ass grin. "You need anything, there's an envelope taped beneath your desk. You can use what's there for office supplies and coffee and snacks. The usual. Okay?" I looked over at Friday and had an afterthought. "And dog treats, too."

She smiled and I shuffled paper to come up with a list of phone numbers. I handed it over before heading for the door.

"When are you coming back?" She didn't look concerned. Only aloof. "You know, in case anyone asks." She looked at me.

Friday perked up his ears and followed her gaze.

I took a second to bask in the attention—the dog's attention, that is.

"If anyone asks, it'll be a client showing up. Lock them in so they can't escape and call me. Otherwise, open at nine and close at five and I'll see you later tomorrow. If you're short of cash till payday, you can use what's in the kitty for necessities."

Before Matilda could come up with an argument, I headed down the stairs. Content to know I had a secretary. So she owned a knife, a handgun, and a dog. Big deal.

At least the dog appeared friendly.

It was late, but I made for downtown and Boyle's office anyway. I wanted to check in personally, to see if he learned anything about Andrea's murder. He wasn't there, so I headed for the bar where I first crossed paths with Diana in the city.

Why would Diana have anything on Andrea? I couldn't figure it. Sure, they had being a server in common. Friends? Not so much. Beyond the meeting in the glades, they didn't know one another.

Could Nicolas junior all of a sudden have issues with the woman? And if he did, what about Bobbie? Nick started out with her in back of the motel at the pool. That came to an end until I figured we needed Nick junior to get to the old man.

Had someone filled Nick in on the old man's involvement with Pilar's death? Maybe someone passed Nick one of the packages I mailed to the press and the feds.

Revenge. It had to be about revenge.

So who had it in for me at the DEA? I worked for them with Kara for too long. Maybe they thought I was a liability now. That I knew too much.

Could they tie me to the missing cash in the old safe house turned into a cartel bank? If they had me for that, they had to have Bobbie, too. If anything happened to her, it would be my fault.

I wheeled around and sat a stakeout behind the DEA building. Too many hours later I packed it in and headed for the office in the dark.

The lights were out. The sign was on. I unlocked the office door. Enough light shining through the window allowed me to make out a form. Fully clothed and fast asleep on the sofa.

Matilda.

The dog was on the floor, sleeping at her feet. Except he wasn't sleeping. He was wide awake and looking me over. He must have been satisfied with what he saw, because he woofed quietly to let me know he was there. His tail waggled before he wheezed and settled back on the floor. I went to the closet for a blanket and arranged it over the sleeping woman. Friday snuffled his approval.

The woman was probably living out of her car. Perhaps now would be as good a time as any to move out of the apartment upstairs.

Come morning I knocked on the office door and announced breakfast. Matilda opened it and looked at me. I'd taken her by surprise. Her hair was in disarray. She tried brushing it into a semblance of order with her fingers. The pistol sat on the arm of the sofa.

She muttered and offered up some excuse about working late. I held up a hand. "Upstairs. The door is open."

She grabbed for her bag and slipped the holstered handgun into it before starting up the stairs. She halted and rushed back for her laptop bag. Maybe she thought she was about to get fired. The dog traipsed after his mistress.

Matilda sat at the kitchen table and Friday plopped down beside her. I couldn't hold back the satisfied smile. The woman wolfed down everything I put in front of her, including seconds. Young Friday managed to get only a little toast with a taste of jam.

"You can clean up in the bathroom. Take a shower if you want. There's towels and a robe in the closet. I'll be downstairs. I'll walk the dog while I wait if that's all right. Later you can take the time and pick up some food for him.

Friday wasn't about moving until Matilda gave a signal. I noticed, too.

He snuffled. I knew she said the words for my ears.

"Friday." The dog's ears perked up. "It's all right," she told him. "Go with Jim."

I circled the block with Friday in tow. Or maybe it was me he had in tow. The dog heeled. He sat and waited patiently at the lights and then walked with me back to the office. Impressed with one another, we entered the office and waited for his mistress to show up for work.

I flipped through yesterday's pictures from the stakeout. Found the clearest one and left it on-screen. Against expectations, Matilda showed up on time. How could she not? All she had to do was walk downstairs.

"I would have shown up early, but you stopped to check the office last night and found me and that excuse flew out the window."

"I get it. It's all right. I'll look for a new place to stay. You can move in when I'm gone," I told her.

"I can't afford a place that good," she said.

"Don't worry about it. It's part of the office. It's pet-friendly, too."

"Whose picture is on the dresser?" she wanted to know.

She must have noticed it while she dressed. "That's Andrea. You're her replacement."

"She's pretty. Were you close to her?"

I knew Matilda would probably be confused by it all. Without Bobbie here to clue her in, I went ahead full speed. Like a car heading toward a cliff. Like the driver didn't know.

"Sort of," I said. "We worked a case together. She was great at it, too."

"Sounds like I have some pretty big shoes to fill."

"Nah. Don't worry about it. You're only here to answer the phone and take messages."

Which, I suddenly remembered, was exactly the same thing I said to Andrea. Maybe I was feeling guilty. So I asked. "You want to come on a stakeout? I'm looking for the man on my phone."

"Friday." She had the dog's full attention. "Say here. I'll be back." She bent to pet him before closing the office door.

Matilda took my phone and flicked her fingers over the keyboard. The photo appeared on her phone's screen. She studied it before heading downstairs.

"We're taking your car," I told her.

She gestured across the street toward an old beater. Green paint. Faded by too much sun and salt air. Back seat filled with paper and plastic bags, some with clothes and others with canned food.

"You've been living in your car."

A bright pink flushed her face. "It wouldn't take a detective to figure that, now, would it? Do you still want me to work for you?"

I wondered how she managed to come up with a permit for the handgun with no fixed address. Maybe she knew someone.

"You need to renew the gun permit. It's about to expire. You can use my address. I'll fill out the paperwork and you can sign it. I'll send it in."

She slipped into the driver's seat and I gave her directions to the DEA building I discovered, thanks to Diana. Nervous, she looked across the seat while I kept the corner of an eye on her. She was a good driver. Even better, the air worked. So did the radio.

I made her take the car around the back of the building. She paid attention while I gave her instructions for pickup if she caught sight of the man in the picture.

I left her in the car by the parking lot while I took up a position on the sidewalk across the street from the front of the building.

It wasn't long before Matilda turned up. I hopped in and she gunned it down the street. "He's in the maroon car. He's got a woman with him," she said.

"Did you get a good look at her?" I asked.

"Tall. Dark hair. Big tits," she said.

I looked at her.

She said, "Well, everyone's tits are bigger than mine. Probably even yours."

"Are you a woman?"

Matilda looked like she wanted to punch me. Her grip tightened on the wheel.

"Of course I'm a woman. What kind of a question is that?"

Considering she answered all my questions during the interview, I supposed she was within her rights to be upset with that one.

"Then you've got everything you need in all the right places. Now drive."

She followed the car at a respectable distance. Matilda did a good job keeping a couple of cars between us. The car halted in front of the bar where I first saw Diana in the city. Matilda drove past and pulled into a side street. She halted on the crosswalk, leaving me a view down the sidewalk.

Diana got out and walked into the bar and I knew we'd hit paydirt. "Good job," I told her. "Now take us back to the office.

"I can't."

"What? Why?"

She checked the rearview. "We're boxed in."

So many badges and guns pointed at us, I thought Matilda might offer her resignation without waiting until we got back to the office.

She handled it well. She kept her hands on the steering wheel and stayed calm but for the beating the wheel took from her thumbs tap-tap-tapping.

I was the unlucky one to get hauled out of the car and escorted into the back of a plain white van. The door slid shut behind me.

"Do you know who you were following?"

I pleaded ignorance, not wanting to answer the question.

"You were following a DEA agent."

"Oh, really? Which one is the agent so I don't make the same mistake again?"

"Very funny. Now give it up and go back to where you came from."

"Well, in that case, my driver will take me home. You want to come along for the ride so you know where that is for future reference?"

"We could haul your asses in."

"For what? Riding around town like teenagers looking at the boys and girls?"

That got him. The door slid open. Matilda was out of the car. Two agents were busy interviewing her, firing questions at her faster than she could come up with answers. She sounded very annoyed.

"No. I was not. You're mistaken. You're making shit up. Now stop trying to bully and intimidate me.

Don't you have the common sense your mother gave you to know that you can't do that any more? Piss off."

I opened the door and climbed in, waiting for Matilda to tie up loose ends. I didn't have to wait long. She was that good at it.

"Good job, partner. Now let's take this dog and pony show back to the office. I think we got what we came for. In fact, we got a lot more than we came for."

And we had. I knew now the DEA was involved. And Diana, whatever role she had, was involved up to her neck. So was the man in the car with her.

Nicolas.

It was a good day. Matilda had proved to be more than capable. She did what she was told. She didn't panic in the face of the three-letter brigade surrounding her car with guns drawn. She kept her cool. I had only one question. "Are you packing?"

"Packing? What? No. I don't have anything to pack. I have it all with me in the car."

"Ah. Of course. Do you need to do laundry?"

"Oh. Yeah. Big time. You got a washer up there? And a dryer?"

"Down the hall. Now show me your sidearm, woman."

"Oh. That kind of packing." Matilda mumbled something. Looked at me, sheepish, before reaching behind to free the S&W. She flipped open the cylinder, palmed the lead, and held it out.

I nodded and watched her load and holster.

"Close enough. You remembered the paper, right? It's almost expired."

She opened her folder-wallet for a look.

"You need to fill out the paperwork for your renewal. The date is getting close. Now where's your driver's license?"

She blushed and looked away. "Umm—"

"We'll work on that later. You want to go to the gun range?"

I didn't wait for an answer. I opened the closet in the office and showed her the sheets and blankets. "You might as well be comfortable. There's a pillow in there, too. I'll start looking for a place tomorrow."

"You don't have to do that. There's a place upstairs, down the hall. When I get paid I'll take it if it's still available."

Matilda wasn't up when I banged on the office door. She cursed before scrambling to get decent. The dog barked. He was doing guard duty, obviously.

"It's only 5:30. I'm not on the clock yet. What do you want?"

"Don't worry. I'm not coming in. Breakfast is ready. Get your ass in gear, woman. The range opens in half an hour."

Matilda rushed past with the worst case of bedhead I ever saw. She hurried up the stairs to the bathroom, bag in hand. The dog trotted after her. He sat down in front of the closed door, looking down the hall. His imposing size made him a good guard dog. The shower turned on. When it turned off, she came out in clean jeans and a long shirt that covered her waist. I already knew what was tucked into the back of it.

"You clean up pretty good."

"Thanks. I think."

"Remind me to give you an advance. You must be running low on clothes by now if you've been living out of that shopping bag."

She flushed a pink even brighter than when I noticed she lived in her car.

"Sorry. I probably shouldn't have said that. It's none of my business."

"My boyfriend tossed me out and changed the locks. I can't get back in. I tried everything. I don't know what to do."

"I can help with that. We'll go after we do the gun range thing."

I convinced her to take the beater. Before we left, I grabbed a big black garbage bag from under the sink and hosed out the coffee cups and other debris littering the floor in front. I left the back for her.

At the gun shop, I introduced her to Harry and he waved us toward the range.

Matilda turned out to be a good shot with the short-barrel hammerless. It was obvious she had training. She used two hands. Kept both eyes open. Squeezed the trigger. Didn't blink or flinch.

"You did good. Now get the paperwork signed. And start working on your driver's license, will you?"

She saluted and gave me a *Yes, boss.*

"When you get it, let me know and I'll pay you mileage whenever you use your car on the outfit's business."

She skipped her way to the car, no doubt counting

the extra cash she would earn.

"Yeah, no. It won't be much. Just get the darned license, okay?"

Hours later, I let Matilda drive me to a small house in the burbs where her ex was holding her furniture hostage. To kill time on the way, I asked plenty of questions. She volunteered the information willingly, like most people when someone bothers to show interest.

Matilda was a country girl from Michigan. Hated winter. Loved summer. Liked dogs. Moved to Florida. Loved it. Got tangled up in a few relationships. Got discarded in the last one. Adopted our business with her dog in tow.

Now we were headed to settle it with her ex and pick up her things. I never could figure how someone could hold someone else's possessions, no matter how much rancor permeated the relationship.

She braked opposite a town house. "This is it. He should be home."

I got out and bent to the window. "Shift work?"

She nodded. "You want me to come with you?"

I scouted the house from across the street. Thick green bushes surrounded the sidewalk on both sides. The only view was directly across the street. Maybe the nosy neighbor would be at work.

"I'll wave you in when it's clear, okay?"

I walked up to the door and knocked politely, not wanting to give it away right off. The door opened and the tall, gangly ex scanned the street.

"Yes? Who're you?"

He didn't recognize Matilda in the car. Maybe the kid didn't see her.

"I'm here for a friend. She wants her things."

The door slammed. The lock twisted. After a wave at Matilda I kicked the door. Wood splintered. The jam shattered.

Matilda advanced, bringing up the rear.

"I'll sit on him while you collect your things."

"Sit on him? You don't have to do that."

"It's an expression. Load up and let's get going. You need me to lay down the law for the boy?"

"Probably wouldn't be a bad idea. He locked me out. It's all my stuff you're looking at."

"Good to know."

I motioned for the kid to approach. "We're coming back with a moving van to pick up the rest of Matilda's things. I suggest you leave a key under the doormat out front. If it's not there, we'll be doing the same to the back door."

I made a show of calling a local moving company. They promised to pick up Matilda's stuff after she sent a list and pictures. I held out the phone for her. "Talk to them if you want to sleep in your own place tonight, Matilda."

"You can call me Maddie if you promise to never call me late for breakfast. Ever." The woman grinned like a kid eating ice cream on a hot day who knew another scoop was on the way.

All of a sudden, I felt like a hero.

If I knew anything, that feeling wouldn't last.

8

Maddie knocked on the door to the apartment and walked in. I could tell she was expecting the usual ready and waiting breakfast. She looked at the table. Checked the stove. Decided to make do with last night's tired coffee.

"No breakfast," she complained. "What's going on? My pants don't fit right any more?"

She twisted around in an exaggerated attempt to get a look at her backside while Friday took his regular seat by the table. He absentmindedly wagged his tail while looking from one of us to the other. It seemed to be his routine now.

"Don't bother. It'll be fine now that you're eating regularly. Are you ever gonna chip in for the groceries since you're getting paid, or what?"

"Do we have an HR department? I think I want to file a complaint."

"It depends. Do you want to report that I'm finally asking you to pay for the free food you've been eating in your boss's home? Or could it be all about the eating regularly comment?" I raised an eyebrow and couldn't help grinning.

"Go check the office phone. Then meet me at the car. We have somewhere we need to be."

"What? It's barely sunrise and you're forcing me to work."

"You should talk to HR about that, too. Make an appointment and I'll see when I can fit you in."

She almost looked as though she believed me.

"Sunrise was hours ago, woman. You have to open your eyes and get out of bed if you want to see it."

Maddie stumbled down the stairs to the office, yawning and mumbling about slave labor in the 21st century. A few minutes later she showed at the car. "No phone messages, boss. But there's—"

There was no time. "Get in the car. We have to go."

"You need—"

"Not now."

"But—"

"I said not now."

"Whatever you say."

Maddie stuffed something into her bag and climbed in. I think she knew slamming the door wouldn't be wise. Contrary to my after-hours banter, I didn't put up with bullshit on the job.

"Where are we going?" she asked.

"We're going to sit outside a bar and see what turns up."

It was barely eight in the a.m. I left Maddie with the car and told her to park out back. I returned to the doorway and the awning across the street where I first spotted Nicolas parking his car before heading into the same bar.

The bar opened at eight. While I didn't think any

but the most dedicated drinkers might entertain the thought of starting at that early hour, it was still a place where anyone could show up for a meeting. Or a first drink of the day before slogging off to the nine-to-five.

The phone pinged. A text from Maddie.

there's a woman. tall. large breasts

nice legs and ass?

i guess if you don't like big tits

diana

if you say so. how do you know for sure? tits or ass?

prior experience

say no more. you going in again?

smartass and yes

Diana frowned and didn't appear so happy when I sat down beside her in the dimly-lit bar. By now she knew I was aware of her DEA cover thanks to yesterday's rousting. She visibly squirmed on the barstool.

"What are you doing here, Jim?" She made sure I caught the side-eye. "Didn't you get the message yesterday?"

So she had been the one to set the dogs on us. "I

might ask you the same thing about your everglades adventure. Last time I saw you, your feet were aimed at the sky."

"That's right. And you know how to spoil a girl's fun, too, don't you?"

"It couldn't have been spoiled for long. I see you're still tangled up with Nick." I tried not to smile as I remembered the image.

"All work and no play for a girl—"

"Yeah, I don't believe that for a minute. You're working him for something," I said. In fact, I was certain.

"You were trying to work me at the yacht club in Diamondhead, too. I didn't fall for it then and I'm not going to now," Diana said. She didn't appear surprised that I'd put it together.

"You know, I read all about you. You've got quite a file."

So that's how the woman was going to play it. "Could be. I'm not privy to anything in my file. Most of it is probably lies and the rest of it shit someone made up. If I remember right, there wasn't a soul in the DEA I could trust when it came right down to it."

"Is that why you quit?" she asked.

If she knew anything, she knew I didn't quit. I was never an employee. "Quit? I wouldn't call it quitting when the outfit pulled the rug out from under me. Supporting their people isn't their strong point, is it?"

I was a contractor. Off the books. One they didn't given a shit about. Diana had to know that, too.

"Too bad about Kara. She was a good agent."

Dragging Kara's name into the conversation wasn't the smartest thing. My relationship with the woman was behind me now. Had been for quite a while.

"Is there anything in my file about her kid's father? I'm sure the little guy will want to know one day."

"The file says it's you."

She was lying and I knew it. "Then the file is sadly mistaken. DNA says otherwise."

Surprise flashed across Diana's face. The surprise disappeared almost as fast as she tried to conceal it. So maybe she wasn't lying after all. Maybe it was in my file. Along with every other falsified report.

"You need to know I'd give just about anything to find out who placed that bit of falsehood in the file." Someone wanted me to feel guilty enough to keep working for them, thus the note left in the file.

"So then, you going to tell me why you're sitting in a bar at eight in the morning? I'm pretty sure you're not that hard up for a drink."

Diana said, "Let's grab a table. Your girl can wait a little longer, I'm sure." She waved the bartender over and ordered a virgin Mary. "Take it out to the little girl in the alley."

Diana settled in the booth with her back against the wall. She swung her long legs up onto the seat. Her ankles stuck out into the aisle. She crossed them and caught me looking. "You always did like them, didn't you?"

"I can't disagree. You didn't invite me here to admire your legs, though. Or anything else. You were going to tell me something. And then you were going to pump me for information.”

“I’ll pump you for more than that if you get rid of your friend in the alley,” Diana said.

“No can do. She’s part of the business now.” Exasperated, I stood up to leave and flipped a card on the table. “If you want to see me, you can make an appointment. Just like anybody else.”

I left and joined Maddie waiting in the car. She was sucking back the drink. “You can take us back to the office.” Somehow, I knew she wouldn’t be giving up that easily.

“So did you get anything?”

“Only that she’d do me if you weren’t around.”

“You want I should catch a bus?”

I caught her expression before she turned to look out the window. Any second she’d be laughing her ass off.

“I don’t think it would have been that immediate. You want me to go back and ask?” I could be a smartass too.

“Nah. She’s top-heavy. If she ever fell on her back, she’d never get up again. Like a turtle. Arms and legs frantic and scratching for air. Going nowhere in a hurry.”

The picture Maddie painted reminded me of Diana’s escapade in the glades where the woman did just that. I couldn’t contain my laughter. “Damn, Maddie. You have a way with words.”

“Yeah, that’s what the boys always said. So, what do we have so far? A DEA agent you slept with—”

“Hey now. Wait just a minute.”

“All righty, then. A DEA agent you want to sleep with. Some bozo in a convertible that’s sleeping with her. A business partner and lover who buggered off and you have no idea if she's coming back. A new girl in the office that hands you shit you take. A dog you like. How am I doing so far?" she wanted to know.

"Well, you got the dog part of it right. My question is, how has old Friday managed to put up with you up to now?"

"I feed him. I walk him. I water him. I rub him. I love him. Kinda like you do with me, minus the last two. So far."

I put up with it to get to the office and then I ran her off up the stairs.

She said, "Take poor old Friday for a walk. I'd go along, but I don't want you getting any ideas."

Friday woofed as Maddie led him to the stairs. I reached to scratch him behind the ears. "Good boy, Friday. Don't let that woman take you for granted. Women like her tend to do that with their men more often than not."

My phone buzzed. Caller ID said it was Diana. I must have given her the card with my personal number scrawled on the back.

I didn't get a word in past *Hello*.

"Don't hang up on me, Nash." She went on before I could interrupt. "We're getting off to a bad start. I'm sorry I tried to make you lose your temper. I was trying to get even for something."

"Anything I should know about?" I asked.

"No. It's nothing. It was in my head. Not any more. I didn't mean to upset you about your son."

That again. "I told you. He's not my son. But

Kara's sister is going to get the question one day. She should know how to answer it, don't you think?" She should definitely know.

"You're right. I'm sorry."

"Stop with the apologizing." The woman could be exasperating. "You want something. What is it?"

"Come by my place tonight, Nash. I should have something for you by then."

If it was information about Erica's nephew, James, I'd be all in. On the other hand— "All right. I will."

Diana texted me what I needed to find her.

I spent the day with Maddie and Friday. She busied herself setting up the office to her satisfaction. She organized a filing system for files we didn't have. Arranged empty cabinets. Fussed with desktop items.

When she was done, I stood back to admire her handiwork. "This calls for a celebration, wouldn't you say?"

I loaded everyone in the Packard and headed for the dog park. Friday rode in the back with his head out the window. If I could have joined him, I would.

"Diana called me earlier." I was trying to be nonchalant.

"That was fast," she said. "You must have really impressed her with your detectiving skills."

Apparently, it wasn't working. "Well—"

"Or you spent the entire time staring at her tits and wishing. She got the message by osmosis."

"Maddie—" She was starting to annoy me. So far,

only slightly.

"So then, what's your deal with that one?" she wanted to know.

"She says she has something for me."

"I'll bet she does."

"No, it's not like that. It's about a boy. He needs to know who his father is."

"Is he your son?" she wanted to know.

I didn't mind when Maddie asked. "Not in the slightest."

"I believe you. Her boy?"

"No. Not hers, either."

We arrived at the dog park and Maddie stopped asking questions. I was relieved.

Friday bounded out the open car door and ran back and forth, anxiously waiting for the Frisbee that would be coming.

Maddie threw, and Friday wrestled me for it before I pretended to lose. We went back and forth until I was a panting, sweaty mess.

The dog was smarter than I was. He knew when he had enough. He plopped down beside me and dropped the Frisbee. I stretched out beside him in the grass. My exhaustion wasn't feigned. "Good dog, Friday. You know when to quit, too."

Maddie shook her head. "You guys. You both need to stop liking your own cooking."

"Friday. Did you hear that? Your mistress thinks you're fat."

"I wasn't only talking about Friday. You have just a bit of a muffin top, too."

"Just a bit, you say?" I gave her the up and down. "You aren't looking so bad since you started eating the free food."

"I know. I wasn't suggesting that you stop cooking for me."

It was my turn to give the woman a head-shaking. "Come on, Friday. Your mother says we're too fat. Let's chase that Frisbee some more. By any chance did anyone bring water for us?"

When it was over, it was time to drop Maddie and her faithful dog Friday at the office. "I have an errand to run. I'll be back in a bit."

"Diana?"

I didn't answer. She was the rookie detective. I'd let her do the detecting.

I found a pet store and picked up a portable water bowl for the dog. The clerk demonstrated how you could fill the bottle, pull open the partial tray, and let the dog gurgle and splash as he drank. For good measure, I threw in a big thick doggie bed for the office.

Friday's tail would probably wag when he spotted the plush bed and settled into it. I already knew Maddie's would when I showed her the water bottle. She loved that dog to death.

I kind of liked both of them.

The light in the office was on and the door was open when I started down the stairs, freshly shaved and showered. I slowed and went into stealth mode. It didn't do any good. Friday sold me out with a loud woof. I'd have to talk to him about that.

"I'll be here if you need me," Maddie assured me. "Call any time."

Shit. The woman was a mind reader. Just for spite, Friday woofed a second time. They were both onto me. "All right. I will."

"No, you won't. Not even when hell freezes over and that woman is wearing a parka and long underwear."

Maddie was probably right about that, too.

I leaned on the buzzer to let Diana know I was there. She let me in after forcing me to wait a suitable amount of time. Her own door was open. Welcoming, even. I'd reserve judgment on that.

She smiled warmly and greeted me with a demure little number that ended at her knees. Loose-fitting. Flowing over the curves lingering beneath. It was the same old Diana I knew, tempting and easy.

"You want coffee? I was just going to make some." Without waiting for an answer, she turned, pushed herself up on tiptoes, and reached for two cups. Well-toned calves stood out courtesy of taut muscle.

I fantasized about the rest of her hidden by the skirt, even though I was familiar with all of it. "Sure. Why not?"

She fussed over a cherry red espresso machine combo. Milk hissed. "You're getting a crema. I hope you like it."

My favorite, but she didn't need to know. For some reason it pleased me that she presented it in a mug. Apparently, she wasn't one for formality when it came to coffee in all of its varieties. She sat down at the opposite end of the sofa and curled long legs beneath her.

"You were surprised by my invitation."

I was, but I wouldn't admit it. I wanted to know what she had—and not the way Maddie told me it would go. Strange how I was thinking about Maddie now.

There was no preliminary. Diana got up and retrieved a file from the kitchen counter. She sat back down and pushed it at me. "Take a look at this."

"What is it?"

"It's the second file on you. You have two."

Incredulous, I looked at her. "What? Two? Why two?"

"I wondered about that too when I started looking around. Apparently, one is for public consumption, to discredit you in case something you do turns to shit. It's not recent. It's all about your past as a free agent with us."

She tapped a second file. "This one is more recent. Apparently, you created quite a fuss when you bumped into Bobbie Dawson and her brother in Diamondhead."

Would that be because Diana was the one who filed the report? After all, she was working in the Diamondhead marina's bar. What part of that had to do with the safe house turned into a stash house? That was probably the DEA's main concern. But since Bobbie and brother were safe and sound, why would it mean anything now? Unless—

"They think you stole money from them."

So, somebody up top was pulling the strings. I wondered how high it went. I went for the coffee mug to mask my surprise. "Who's dirty?" I wanted to know.

"I don't know yet."

Yet. There was no hesitation. It was obvious she was assigned to work on it.

"I'm doing it on my own," she said.

Okay, so Diana wasn't assigned to it. She was off book. That was a no-no if ever there was one. An agent going rogue, off the rails, could lead to sudden death, Mexican style. Those fine legs wouldn't look so good parted out from the main attraction.

I regarded Diana with renewed interest. Perhaps she wasn't so evil after all. "Are you crazy? They'll flay you alive if you make one wrong move. One wrong half-step. A dance step to the wrong tune. Damn, Diana. You're playing with fire."

So far, I hadn't opened the file. Finding out that she was rogue was a major distraction. I placed it on the coffee table. Diana shifted. Thighs brushed. She may not have noticed, but I did. She was still capable of affecting me, and not in a good way. I'd be lucky to get out of this place before sunrise if I wasn't careful.

Then there would be Maddie to deal with.

I paged through the file, speed-reading. I stopped when I had to take more time over the unintelligible handwritten scrawl by someone whose name I didn't recognize.

Diana's warm thigh pressed against mine. She leaned in to point out things I didn't catch. It seemed like I was getting warmer each time she did it. It felt good.

"Why are you doing this?" I asked.

She didn't sit up to look at me. She kept going through the file, telling me things I didn't know they kept in files any more. "I need your help. It's too much for me. I can't trust anyone in the agency."

"No one?" I asked for effect.

"That's right. No one."

Her hand rested on my thigh, but it wasn't remotely an attempt at seduction. The look on her face was one of desperation. And she knew about the beef with DHS to boot. It was all in the file.

She flipped to the back of the thick document. The submission on Pilar's death was there, recorded, stamped, and initialed. It didn't appear as though anything beyond that had been done with it. That realization was all it took.

"All right. I'll help. But I have conditions."

Diana's intake of breath was palpable. She made it sound almost like a *thank goodness I found somebody*, minus the words. The hand that was inexorably tightening its grip on my thigh relaxed and withdrew.

"Thank you, Nash. I don't know what I would have done if you refused."

Diana didn't move away. Our thighs still touched. Her hand went back to where it was, as though in a caress. Her eyes moved to mine, unsure of whether to continue. "Would you— do you want— can we—"

"Yes to all three."

She stood up and walked down the hall to the bedroom. "I'll be right back."

"No. You don't have to. But if you do, I'll be glad to help," I said.

"I want you to see what I was going to wear until I thought better of it."

"I'm glad you thought better of it. Maybe you could wear it for me in the morning."

There was just enough light coming through the

bedroom door to allow me to see the parts of the woman I hadn't yet been privy to. I took my time with all of them.

A sweaty sheen covered Diana. It ended up all over me. My hands moved easily over her, slipping and sliding, testing and feeling and enjoying.

"No more, Nash. For once I've had enough. And stop that grinning."

"I was remembering something about you."

"Here we go. Already you're throwing my past in my face."

"You bet I am. I seem to recall—"

"I know what it is, too. It's about what I told you at my place in Diamondhead, isn't it? Well, I changed my mind. It's a woman's prerogative."

I threw it back at her. "Your house, your rules."

"In that case, I want you in my house and obeying my rules."

She slipped a leg over and settled without hesitation. She moaned. Rocked back and forth faster and faster. Her lips whispered *my house, my rules* rhythmically in my ear until she stopped making sense and cried out. Sated, she fell off and collapsed on the sweaty sheets. She draped a long leg over mine, wanting me to know she wasn't finished.

"That was quick," I said.

"I wanted to wait. I couldn't."

"Well don't feel bad. I'm sure I'll be in the same situation before long."

"Good. I like knowing I can make a man want only one thing," she said.

Breakfast came late, too. Diana presented herself wearing what she first wanted to wear last night. Everything got served up cold. Only her body was warm beside mine.

"I'm glad I waited to wear this. It would have been wasted last night."

"Now you know I can want only one thing from you, too," I said.

"I'm going to enjoy knowing how you want me."

Maybe she was right. But I didn't know if I'd ever come back. "Thanks for showing me the file. Now can you somehow find out who scribbled the unreadable stuff? I'm pretty sure whoever it was didn't want to be found."

"I'll try. Do you want to stay for a shower?"

"Only if you're willing."

She was, and I was.

Maddie would have to wait.

9

I **observed Maddie wandering** aimlessly around the office, wordlessly picking things up and putting them down. I got the distinct impression she was disappointed with me, but only because she would look at me and then look away.

"You leaving your scent behind?" I wanted to keep it light.

"Not particularly." She looked absently at the huge sign in the window.

"Where's the Dawson part of the fancy neon, Nash?"

Maddie had to have heard the sigh. It was just as well she pretended not to. "She seems to have disappeared from my life. Last I saw, she emptied the bedroom of clothes into a bag and headed out for parts unknown."

Maddie sat down at Bobbie's old desk and pretended to contemplate life. It was my turn to look out the window to mask my distress.

"I like your mural. Who painted it?"

"The woman you replaced. Andrea. I'm living in her apartment."

"Ah."

Wisely, she left it alone, perhaps suspecting Bobbie left because of that. "So, what happened to her?"

More questions. Women asked too many questions. Even the ones I liked. "She was murdered."

Her head turned toward me so fast it displaced her short hair. "Your partner? What happened?"

"No. Andrea."

"Who murdered her? Your partner? Was she jealous?"

"No. She was fine with it." As far as I knew.

"She was fine with you and another woman? I don't think you understand women in the slightest."

I knew that to be too true. I ignored her and instead took a look at my pinging phone. A text from Diana, wanting to meet. An address I didn't recognize stared back.

"Diana?"

I had to give the girl credit. She knew all about the women in my life. "How did you know?"

She rolled her eyes.

I said, "Maybe you can hold a class later and teach me. I'm not good at tests, though."

She snickered. "I can tell. Your report card is written all over the expression on your face. You want me to wait in the car for you in case it's a honey trap?"

It was my turn for the rolling eyes. "Very well. I'm going home."

"You're already home. You live upstairs, remember?"

"Exactly. Text me if you have questions or need

pointers, but only if it's an emergency. Class will start at 9 a.m. tomorrow. Good night."

Still the smartass. "Right after that HR thing. Did you remember to make an appointment?" she asked.

Women. I stared after Maddie's disappearing form as she bounded up the stairs. Friday hesitated, as if saying he wanted to stay a while and chat. Finally, the dog pulled up stakes and joined his mistress, already halfway up the stairs.

I yelled after both of them. "Your jeans are getting tighter."

The woman didn't skip a beat. "Is that your way of saying you like my ass? I'll be talking to HR tomorrow, remember?"

I propped my feet up on the desk just as she poked her head around the door.

"Good night."

My feet slipped and thumped onto the floor. The chair tipped and then righted itself with no help from me. "Damn, Maddie."

She turned and climbed the stairs a lot slower.

Five minutes later, I locked the office door and headed upstairs for a quick shower to prepare for the visit with Diana. I checked the phone before leaving.

i'm at home. i brought something you need to see. it's waiting. so am i

A text from Maddie pinged. I wanted to ignore it. Knew better.

if you need rescuing i'm available

I sent one right back.

you should probably use the time to prepare for your meeting with hr first thing in the morning

i'll be in the office at my usual time. somehow, I don't think you'll be untangling Diana's legs until brunch if you're still alive by then

smartypants

my pants are just fine, thank you very much. it's yours that are going to need mending after she tears them off

in that case bring a needle and thread to the hr meeting

I turned the phone off and tossed it on the seat. I had time to think about what Diana might have. Surely she wouldn't lure me to her place under false pretenses after last night.

On the other hand, maybe Maddie was right. I turned the phone back on. A text came through immediately.

you turned your phone off, didn't you

okay so maybe you already know her better than i do. i'll keep you posted, all right?

:)

Emoticons. She must have thought I didn't know any beyond the obvious. I should probably learn a few. I turned off the volume and the backlight.

I knew that much.

Diana's voice carried through the door, announcing she would be a few minutes and forcing me to wait.

I twiddled my thumbs until she opened it wide and smiled. I was reminded of the image I had of her splayed out for Nicolas junior back in the swamp. I frowned and walked past the woman to the kitchen. If circumstance had been different—

My eyes homed in on a file, open on the counter.

"You can look as much as you want but you can't take it, all right?" she said, and I wondered if it was a double entendre.

She left and went down the hall, probably to change into something more comfortable. I made a mental note to tell Maddie I wasn't so stupid after all. And then wondered. *How did Diana get the file so fast? Did she have it delivered? Had she been to the office already?* I'd have to remember to ask.

At first it wasn't so easy to step into the past. It got easier the more I read. I shut out everything and immersed himself in the DEA's detailed interpretation of my life since I began working off-book for them.

I thumbed through the beginning pages in a rush. It was all about the early days in Mexico. I didn't need any reminders how that went. A giant screw-up from the beginning. Agents turned. Killed. A traitor in our midst revealed.

Toward the middle of the file, the bulk of it got into Kara. It included only some of her background. How they turned her onto me. To convince me to keep working for them.

Someone liked my work ethic.

There were handwritten notes from Kara. Asking to be relieved of working cases with me. Something about emotional involvement and trust and using someone in love with her. My file, her emotional involvement. Why was that even in the file?

So she loved me after all. Then why pretend to get married? There was no pretending about her pregnancy. It was more than obvious. And why the hell did she blow up the boat?

I pushed the file away. Closed it without finishing. So far, there was nothing of value. I wasn't able to find her handler's name in the stack of paper. That's what I wanted. Her handler. And from him I'd learn who the father of her child was. Maybe it was the handler.

Diana's warm breath was a reminder there was someone else in the room. Her breasts pressed my arm. I turned to face her. She looked damn fine in the sheer blouse that was incapable of hiding her unfettered breasts. I didn't have to get her naked to know what they looked like. She aimed them and arched her back. I didn't try to hide the long, wide-eyed look.

"Did you see what you came to see?"

I didn't think she had the same thing in mind. "I was looking for Kara's handler. I didn't see his name anywhere in that file."

She returned to press urgently against me. It was more than obvious she was ready, and she wanted me that way, too. I obliged by following her to the bedroom. I didn't need a light to see what I was getting into. In the dark room, hands and the rest of my body did all the seeing I needed.

This wasn't any kind of relationship I wanted. Yet here I was, in the dark, literally and figuratively, and in bed. I pushed off of a woman I only wanted to use. This wasn't the way I wanted to use her.

I needed to get out. The sooner, the better. I thought about all the excuses to make an escape. I came up with exactly none. Then the phone pinged.

blah blah blah breakfast or a late brunch??? what's it going to be

Talk about timing.

breakfast your turn to cook

desperate after all are you?

:)

If she could do it, I could too.

Diana twigged immediately. "Is that your new girl? Are you sleeping with her yet? You must be if you're going to rush out of my bed to hers."

"Maybe if you had something new I wouldn't be leaving." What the hell was I thinking? "There isn't a thing in that file that I don't already know. Bring me something new and I'll think about it."

Still, I'd need to see the file again. Too soon I had given up in frustration and stopped reading. I traded it for sex. Maybe it was because of Kara and everything that came flooding back when I was reminded by the report's clinical manner.

I put my arms around Diana and kissed her on the mouth, long and hard and eager. She pressed the long length of her body to me. Wanting me to know I could have her again. I eased my way out of bed to search in the dark for my clothes. She didn't turn on a light. I was tasked with finding them on my own.

"Come back when you want."

So much for the *my house, my rules, now get out* she'd flung at me in Diamondhead.

"I'll need the file. I'm not finished with it."

Was that the excuse? In the dark bedroom, Diana's sigh sounded pleased. I'd given her a reason for my return. She'd be able to take another run.

I closed the apartment door and rushed to the lobby. I almost crashed into Maddie, fresh-faced and grinning up a storm.

"Funny we should be meeting like this. Peeping is against the law."

Maddie made a grab for my arm and dragged me down the steps. "How could you possibly know I was peeping? She has nice breasts. Among other things. Why did you turn her down?"

This could be trouble. Maddie arrived too late to the party to see me traipsing after a woman, bound for her bed.

"So you were peeping. I'm sure your HR officer is going to frown on that. What time is the meeting again? I don't want either of us to be late."

Maddie settled in for the rest of the evening at my place. I didn't mind. I put an old film noir into the player and flashed up some popcorn in the microwave. We traded hands back and forth in the bowl. Reaching. Touching sometimes. Eating.

I was comfortable in my chair. Maddie fell asleep half-way through the movie. True to her word, in the morning she fixed breakfast. It wasn't half bad. The woman could actually cook. As penance, I did the dishes.

"Did I remember to tell you you're hired?"

She reached around to put a plate away. Was I imagining it, or was she brushing up against me on purpose? She did it several times and I didn't mind in the slightest. With the dishes done, she stopped at the door. "You going home?"

I wasn't so sure that was her plan.

"Why don't you make sure I get there safe and walk with me?"

Poor Friday didn't know where to look. He whined and settled in by the sink, where the trouble started. I should get him a bed for my place, too.

"Well, there goes the HR meeting."

She smiled and waited by the door. "We can have it at my place. Bring a notebook. And take a shower. I can smell her on you."

I woke up in an empty bed. Sometimes I had that effect on a woman. On the other hand, Maddie's bed was comfortable and it smelled so damned good beneath the sheets. I checked again, reaching out a hand. Searching. Not expecting to find anything. A hand brushed against something warm and soft and appealing. It definitely wasn't Friday.

I knew, because there was a hint of hair where the hand ended up. It was cropped a lot shorter, too. "You're not gone. I thought you might have left already." It was starting to look like we were both going to be late to the office.

"What are you doing? Stop it. You can't. I need—"

I outmaneuvered her feeble attempt at curling up under the covers. "No you don't. Not yet. Not until I need whatever it is you need."

Maddie sighed and gave up and with her hands and with the rest of her body convinced me not to stop.

Maddie was already dressed. I was disappointed. "You showered without me." Could she tell how much?

"I did. I'm not ready to reveal my best side just yet."

"From what I could tell beneath the covers, all your sides are the best ever."

She blushed and I grinned and she kissed me on the cheek. Rubbed the back of her hand against my face. Why did every woman I knew do that?

"You need a shave. I'll see you at the meeting."

I couldn't find a razor, so I did the *come as you are* thing after a quick shower. I didn't bother taking the time to stop at home for a clean shirt.

"Everyone will know you're doing the walk of shame with yesterday's wrinkled shirt. Do you think they'll know it was my fault?"

Maddie blocked the office door, rubbed my face again, and kissed me on the cheek.

"What a nice way to say good morning."

"Don't push it. We haven't had the HR meeting yet. Did you learn anything?"

I grinned a shit-eating grin, huffed out my chest, and leaned back against the desk. "I sure did. I learned my workmate has a crush."

"It better be reciprocated and not because that big-breasted woman rubbed them all over you before you dumped her and rubbed your body all over mine. And, I own a gun."

So she saw it after all. Suitably chastened, I sat down. "Come here." I pulled her onto my lap. "Take some shorthand."

She went to reach for the notepad but I wouldn't let her.

"Dear Maddie, it has come to my attention that you harbor some doubt as to your boss's true intentions toward you. You will be pleased to know that he will clean off his desk at any time for further discussion concerning these matters yours truly—"

The chair tipped and we ended up on the floor in a tangle of arms and legs. Friday only looked at us, cocked his head, and wandered out the open office door and back upstairs.

"When I asked you if you learned anything, I wanted to know if Diana had anything for you besides her breasts."

I helped her up and straightened the chair.

"They're not that big. Are they? And no. She showed me my DEA file. The original."

"Hers are bigger than mine. You have more than one file? How does that work?"

"Yours are perfect and just what I need. I don't know. There wasn't really anything in it. I wanted to find out who my ex-wife's handler was."

"What a sweet thing to say. Your ex-wife? Bobbie?" she asked.

"You're welcome. How could I want anything else after last night? No. Not Bobbie."

"You certainly know how to flatter a girl. Then who was it?"

"It's not flattery when it's true. Someone who worked for the DEA. We weren't actually married, although I was led to believe we were. I'll tell you about it another time."

The temperature in the office was starting to warm. I had to do something to get us out of the close quarters before we ended up on top of the desk.

"Come on. We're going to the gun range."

Was I willing to admit that Diana could end up being a threat? I hoped not, for Maddie's sake. I already knew Maddie could shoot. Perhaps by letting her vent at the range she wouldn't end up taking pot-shots at me. Or Diana.

"Can we go upstairs first?"

Not exactly what I had in mind when I mentioned going to the gun range. "We just came from there."

"That we did. Can we do it on the office sofa then?" she wanted to know.

"What about the gun range?"

She started unbuttoning her jeans. "We could probably do it there, too. If you want. I'd be willing to try."

We were struggling to get back into our clothes when a knock sounded on the office door. Maddie giggled and opened it. I was still tucking in my shirt.

"Sorry to disturb you, Nash. I thought you'd want to see this."

It was Boyle. He looked from me to Maddie and back again with a huge shit-eating grin stuck on his face. Maddie turned beet-red. I was pretty sure I turned the same color.

"Warm in here, is it?"

It was warm all right. "Detective Boyle, meet my new assistant, Maddie. She's licensed and she carries."

Maddie pulled the holster from behind her back and was about to remove her revolver and unload it before handing it over.

"That won't be necessary, Maddie. If Nash trusts you, I do, too."

Boyle took the envelope from an inner pocket and waved it.

"Do I need to look at it right away? We were just heading to the range. Maybe you'd like to come along."

Boyle said, "I would, but I'm on duty. Maybe next time."

He smiled at Maddie. Friday woofed his approval. So the dog had been a witness to our office indiscretion. When did he come back?

"A woman and a dog. Nash, I'm impressed. You're turning out to be a regular person after all. Nice to meet you, miss. I hope to see you and Nash together again sometime soon." Boyle turned and walked out of the office before returning and sticking his head past the door.

"I almost forgot, Jim. I need to take the painting. Evidence."

Boyle approached the painting.

I wasn't real happy to know he'd be carting it away.

"No I'm not going to explain. Don't worry, you'll get it back." Boyle tugged on the gloves and carefully removed the painting from the wall before leaving.

"I think Boyle approves. I know for a fact Friday does. He was here the whole time and didn't say a word."

Maddie went beet red all over again. She seemed to do that a lot. "Men. Now I have two of you to scratch."

Friday plopped down beside her and she reached to scratch behind the dog's ears. "Your turn, Nash," she said.

"Not on your life. You're not above using a dog to show a man how you can look after him. And I don't like to be scratched behind the ears."

"I noticed. You like to have your back scratched. Diana's handiwork on the left side? I did mine on the right."

So she noticed. It was my turn to turn red and fumble a response. "Damn, Maddie. I'm sorry."

"It's all right. You're working a case, after all. Was it safe sex with her?"

"That's the only kind I'd ever have with that woman," I admitted.

"In that case, maybe we can do what we did more

often now that I know."

"We're going to the range. Now," I ordered.

"Maybe we could stop for more condoms on the way."

She was a practical girl, too.

10

I **introduced Maddie to** Harry, the gun range owner and former big-city cop, now retired. With the formalities over, he asked to see her piece. She hauled it out. Flipped open the cylinder. Dumped the lead into her hand before handing it over, grip first. Harry appeared pleased. He handed over boxes of cartridges for the five-shot and my automatic. Maddie wandered off to check out the store.

"Are you going to shoot it?" Harry asked.

"Yeah. I figured she might as well get familiar. I wouldn't want to surprise her unannounced. It might scare the pants off the woman."

Harry looked around for Maddie, and spotted her by the knife cage. He lowered his voice. "Judging by the way she looks at you, I don't think it would take much."

Thankfully, Maddie was out of earshot, or tomorrow's HR meeting would take a beating for sure. I shook a finger at Harry. "Come on now. I'm trying to turn over a new leaf."

He buzzed us into the pistol range, and I set Maddie up at a table before I emptied a couple of stock magazines. I released the last mag and set my hardware on my table and went to stand behind Maddie as she reloaded.

I let her go through a couple of loads without commenting. She was good. She hit what she aimed at. I corrected her a couple of times with a gentle touch to an elbow and another to her grip. She went along. Her aim improved, if that was possible. I found I didn't have concern about her abilities at the range.

"You're doing great," I told her. "I'm impressed." It wasn't a lie. "Now come and stand behind me. There's one more thing I want to show you." My oversize mags were laid out on the table.

She knew right away the instant she saw them. "Those aren't legal."

"No. But you need to see this. Just in case. Okay?"

She nodded curtly. "Hang onto something in case you pee your pants. If you do, don't be ashamed. You wouldn't be the first."

I pushed a magazine into the grip and dialed in full auto.

"Yeah yeah. Give me a reason," she said.

I took my standard grip. It was one I perfected to prevent the automatic from heading for the sky once the trigger was locked down. I took careful, calculated aim to allow for the recoil.

"Shit. What are you doing, Nash? Your grip is all wrong. You can't hit anything with a grip like that," she insisted.

I squeezed the trigger. The magazine emptied in seconds. I released and replaced and squeezed again. I even hit the target with a couple of rounds. "It's been a while. I'm sloppy. Would you like to try?"

"Would I? No shit, Sherlock. I'm game. Load me up."

We finished reloading. I briefed her on what to expect when she pulled the trigger. "It's heavy with the oversize mag. As soon as you nail down the trigger, it's going to pull up. Grab your wrist. Be careful the slide doesn't cut your hand."

"I'm concerned about the weight. And the grip is a lot larger. My hand is small compared to yours."

"You're right. You'll have trouble hanging onto it if you don't pay attention. You're going to have to hang on tight.," I warned her.

I stood behind Maddie and put my arms around her. She turned her head to look up at me and kissed me on the cheek. My grin was so huge even Harry got on the horn.

"I saw that, you two. Nash, you're in big trouble."

I tried to keep a straight face. My hands gripped overtop Maddie's. She didn't complain. She knew she'd have trouble controlling the weapon from the start.

"Ready?"

"You bet I'm ready, Jim."

"On my mark, okay? 3, 2, mark."

Maddie squeezed the trigger. Lead flew. Brass scattered. I allowed the handgun to wander, wanting her to get a feel for it. I clamped down hard at the end of the first magazine to steady her until the noise stopped."

In the ensuing silence, Maddie released the mag, racked, and checked the action. "Empty and clear. You didn't say *one*."

"I never do. Remember that."

She placed the Model 17 on the table in front of her. Harry's voice carried over on the p.a. "Let me know when I can open."

"One more magazine, Harry," I told him. "Then we'll put it away."

Maddie repeated the exercise. This time I had her squeeze the trigger in bursts. It turned out to be a lot more controllable for her that way. More accurate, too.

The magazine emptied. She released it and placed it on the table. After checking it, she placed her handgun beside it, turned, and surrounded me with her arms. "You're the best, Nash. That HR meeting is going to go really well later tonight."

I left the automatic with Harry to stash in his gun safe. I was getting a little shy about it now that I'd confirmed Diana was DEA and had a hard-on for me. Woman scorned be damned. No way did I want a reason for the feds to start paying attention.

Which was probably a part of the reason the flashing red and blues in the rearview didn't let up, even as I pulled over. The officer stuck his head partway in the window. Eyes wandered through the vehicle, front and back.

"Officer, I have—" Maddie began.

The officer cut her off. "Shut up."

"You need—" She tried again.

"I told you to shut up, lady. Now shut up."

Maddie looked at me and shrugged and did as the nice police officer told her to. Then it was my turn. "Officer—"

"You shut your mouth, too, wiseguy. When I

want shit from you, I'll tase you."

I looked at Maddie and returned her shrug. "Well, we tried. It's all we can do until officer dumbass gets his shit together and acts in a professional manner. Officer—"

"I thought I told you to shut up," he repeated.

That was good enough for me. "You need to know that everything you say is being recorded on video. The feed is live to the internet and is being uploaded as I speak. In other words, it's real time, officer asshole. Now what was it you wanted, exactly? Were I you, I'd make it very plain. And very polite."

I gave him a chance. It was the best I could do before making a request. The look on the cop's face was priceless. "Are you seeing what I'm seeing, Maddie?"

"You betcha. Can't miss it. Looks to me like officer dumbass is gonna have some 'splainin' to do when he gets back to the unemployment line-up."

I addressed the cop. "I'd like a supervisor. Immediately. While you're waiting, was there something you actually wanted with me, or were you just being a patsy for a buddy?"

It became plain that the cop was reconsidering. I wanted to let it go, too, but something got under my skin. "Any ETA on that supervisor? He needs to know what's going to be on his plate for the next few days as the video gets views. It's on a popular watchdog site. There's not much chance he'll miss it."

I decided to keep running with it.

"In fact, I expect my phone will start ringing any minute now with the press looking for a quote.

Would you like to give them one?"

My phone chose exactly that instant to ring. Luck was on my side, after all. By the time I passed the phone out the window, officer stupid retreated to the comfort of the air-conditioned black and white.

"Is it really the press?" An incredulous Maddie asked.

"Nah. It was Harry. We forgot your ammo on the counter."

The super took his time showing up, but when he arrived, I was able to convince him I would show up at the precinct with the video in hand. He thanked me and we were gone.

We weren't done for the day by any stretch. Two very large men were waiting for us at the office. They patted us down and relieved Maddie of her revolver. "The message we came to pass on is that you should give it up. Whatever you're doing, stop it now. If you don't, the consequences very well could be dire."

"Have you got a card in case I need to call later? I need a meeting with my client first," I told them.

For my trouble, I took one to the gut that put me down on my knees. While I was there, Maddie managed to get a shoulder into the other one. He smacked her and knocked her head backwards. She fell onto her back on the sofa. A knee in her stomach kept her down and out of breath.

"This should help you decide," dumbass number one said.

I took another one to the side of the head. It sent me sprawling onto the floor. Maddie aimlessly kicked her legs and tried getting up. She failed. The goon riding herd on her was too big.

I came to with my head cradled in Maddie's arms. She was sobbing, rocking back and forth. Tears streamed down her face. She snuffled and kissed me and I was able to taste her salty tears.

"You can let me go now. I'm only going to have a king size headache for a little while."

She walked me upstairs and down the hall to her bedroom and crawled in beside me. "You want anything?"

"I already have it," I told her and settled in.

She adjusted her position with her head on my arm. "Good. Me too."

"When did we get naked? I don't remember."

"Are you having memory problems? The first time, or this time? If you are, I need to keep you awake."

She pressed her breasts against my face, and suddenly I was too busy to remember.

M orning came far too early, even if I was waking up in Maddie's bed.

"Get up you lazy lump. It's time for breakfast," she insisted. Friday barked. He obviously agreed.

I groaned and eased out of bed. "I don't know what hurts more, my bruises or the parts of me you happen to like," I complained.

"If that were true, you'd be sore all over. Now get busy and get down the hall. Sustenance awaits."

"Maddie, we need to talk," I told her.

"Oh-oh. Here it comes. Which talk are we having? The relationship talk? The *it's-too-soon-after-the-last-woman-in-my-life* talk? The *we-need-*

time-apart talk? Or will it be the *this-is-getting-too-serious-and-we-need-to-take-a-break* talk?"

"No. None of the above," I insisted. "Actually, I'm happy, in case you can't tell. I hope you are, too. I think you're amazing. And I like the way we work together. And I hope you never get so fed up with me that you pack all your things in a bag and leave."

"Yeah. Me too. Now what was it you wanted to really talk about?"

She wriggled out of her jeans in front of me and sat in my lap.

"That's very distracting when I'm trying to be serious."

"Well, in that case, if I go into the bedroom and crawl beneath the sheets, you won't be so distracted, will you?"

I took her hands and pulled her arms away. She stood up. She didn't replace the jeans. She began to clear the table while I ran water in the sink for the dishes.

"There's something going on. That traffic stop yesterday was meant to go wrong. We weren't breaking any laws."

"I agree. If you didn't have the camera—"

"There is no camera. I made it up on the spur of the moment. I figured it would cool his jets, and it did. Someone has passed the word around to do whatever they need to get to us."

With cleanup finished, I disappeared. By the time Maddie came looking, I was in bed.

"This is a new one on me. I don't remember ever having dessert after breakfast."

She finished undressing and climbed in beside

me, fresh and warm and happy.

"Well, since you came into my life carrying the help wanted sign, a lot of things have changed for the better. We're going for a walk as soon as we're done."

It took a while for the walk to arrive. Eventually we struggled to make our way downstairs. Friday knew the walk word. I wasn't surprised. He was waiting by the door.

"We're looking for a convertible. And what might be parked close to it."

Maddie took my hand. Friday approved. He stuck his wet nose to our interlocked fingers and licked. "In case you haven't noticed, detective, this is Florida. Every third car is a convertible."

"No, no. It's a vintage convertible," I said.

"All righty then, every fourth car."

"This one is a Cadillac. A boat. Early 70s. Maroon exterior. Maroon and white interior. It actually looks pretty good. It's in pristine condition."

"What's so special about it?" she wanted to know.

"It belongs to a friend of Diana's. I think she might be running him. Or he's running her. It's a toss-up. We need to see what other cars might be in the vicinity. I want to know if I know any of them."

Maddie hauled out her phone. "If we find it, we can look at the pics later to see if we missed anything."

"It sure would be nice if we could get access to the CCTV monitors in the street."

"Sorry, boss. Can't help you there."

I recognized the car right away. It was the same one I used to drive Andrea out to the everglades. Andrea with the deep blue eyes and freckles and sense of humor. The one I was with—Maddie—wasn't far off that, either. Maybe I had a type after all.

"This is the one. He's here somewhere." I showed her the picture on my phone.

"Keep your eyes open. You've already seen Diana."

"Show me one of her, too." Maddie said. "I only saw her through the curtain." She took the phone and scrolled through Jim's images.

"I see you managed to get her breasts in more than a few."

"Just so you know. I didn't put them there," I said.

She held out my phone and I took it back.

"Do you think you'll ever have any of me on your phone? I might consider taking my top off for you."

"I'm not sure HR would approve. I'll have to think about it, since I saw you in just that condition only an hour ago. In fact, I can still see you."

Maddie blushed and smiled and muttered while I made a note of Nick's plate number. "I'll see you back here in an hour. Be safe."

We separated, on the lookout for the duo. There were plenty of bars and restaurants and patios. Plenty of meeting places. Any one of a dozen could be the one. I went for the out-of-the-way spots. Patios with shades and screens where business could be done without prying eyes and ears.

I got lucky about twenty minutes in. I recognized a voice and discovered Nick and Diana and another couple in heated discussion. Plenty of hand and arm waving and frustrated gestures.

I texted Maddie the location and she joined me on

the down-low. "I got here as fast as I could." She was out of breath.

"You take the other couple," I said. "If they separate, stay with the guy. I'll handle Nick and Diana."

"I'll bet you will, too," she said. She was grinning. It was all good.

"We'll meet back at the office."

The couples split up. Maddie followed the strangers. I stuck to Nick and Diana like a wet t-shirt until they ended up at Nick's convertible. Diana got in and they took off. I noticed she didn't spend any time slipping across the seat. Were they finished that way?

I headed to the office to wait for Maddie. At dark, I locked up and headed upstairs. I put an old noir in the player and fell asleep watching Bogart and Bacall clean up gangsters in Key West.

At midnight, Maddie still wasn't home. I knew, because I checked her apartment. Now I was worried for real until footsteps sounded on the stairs. Maddie fell through the door. I caught her as she was about to collapse.

"What happened? Are you all right?" I carried her to the bedroom.

"I followed them to a van. They separated. I tried to stick with the guy but he disappeared. Someone jumped me. The next thing I know, I'm being dragged back to the van. The woman is gone. They loaded me in the back and I got twenty questions." Maddie was exhausted.

"What did they want to know?"

"They asked about Bobbie and Andrea and you

and who you were working for. I couldn't lie. I didn't know anything. So that's what I told them. Next thing I know they slid open the door and dumped me a couple of blocks away."

"I'm glad you're okay, Maddie."

She stripped and headed for the shower. I wanted to follow, but when the invitation didn't come, I jumped ship and headed for the office. Maddie showed up minutes later, fresh out of the shower. "I thought you'd be down here when I didn't find you. What's going on?"

I was forced to level with her. "You need to know that we don't have a client. I'm working for myself. Something happened a long time ago that I had thought I put behind me. It hasn't work out that way."

"So after all the years, you're starting fresh and it's been too long and you don't know what the hell happened in the interim," she said.

"Yeah. Something like that. First Andrea. Then Bobbie. And now you kidnapped." I was worried.

"At least they brought me back."

"I'm afraid for you, Maddie. Maybe—" I began.

"No. I'm not leaving. But I'm also not leaving my piece behind ever again, even if you ask me to," she said.

"Your first reaction was to go for it, wasn't it?" I was pretty sure I knew the answer.

"Oh yeah. You have no idea how disappointed I was when it wasn't there."

"Probably just as well. Boyle wouldn't be happy filling out all the paper you'd have forced on him."

Someone was trying to get to me. Someone I knew, most likely. It had to have something to do with the contract work I did for the DEA. But who and why? Kara? No chance. She was dead and out of my life. Andrea, murdered in the office? Bobbie who had up and deserted? Maddie had been kidnapped and returned.

And all for what? What did I know that was capable of getting people killed? Who was doing the killing? Who wanted to torture me by making sure the people in my life disappeared? Was it jealousy? Kara had loved me, so she said. Yet she was pregnant by another man. Had I been the one to take her away before even she knew she was pregnant? Did James' real father know?

And all this after so many years passed. What was responsible for bringing back ancient history at this late date? And now Maddie was involved.

"Maddie? We need to talk."

She wasn't having any of it, of course. Even when I explained the help wanted sign she claimed for her own was supposed to be for an office drone. Answer phones. Type. Take notes. The usual boring stuff in a detective's office.

"It's too late now, Jim. I'm involved. Whether or not you like it. Are you coming upstairs to bed, or are you sleeping on the sofa?"

If the stern look was any indication, I knew where I had to be. I joined forces with Friday and met Maddie in the bedroom, beneath the sweetest smelling sheets ever. Well, okay, so Friday didn't get between the sheets. He knew better.

I brought everything to bed. Before long, Maddie

was sitting up, trying to help me figure it out. "Talk about bringing work home. Isn't that what breaks couples up?" I asked.

"I sure hope not, or you'll be getting the boot, Detective Nash."

I considered myself told.

11

I didn't wake up any the wiser, even after last night's fretting in bed. Whatever was going on, I was completely out of the loop—if there even was a loop. Bobbie. Andrea. Diana. Maddie. The only one I was certain about was Friday, and I had no idea where the dog fit into my life. Although, I did have a glimmer that Friday would be departing with Maddie when she left.

Friday was her dog, after all, and I would end up back where I started—nowhere.

Andrea, who accompanied me to the everglades to rescue Bobbie, ended up murdered in the office. I was no farther ahead on that one. Although, I did have my suspicions. I was at the point where I would give that one up to Boyle. I was too close to the victim.

Bobbie's missing clothes and her bag told me she took off for parts unknown. Could I blame her? She had to be spooked by Andrea's murder.

All disappeared. *Desaparecidos*, as the Mexicans called it. Minus the parting out.

With everyone I cared about gone, I was forced to

hire someone to answer the phone. Thus Maddie came on the scene holding the help wanted sign I taped to the ground-floor window. She was a positive addition. Her dog, Friday, certainly didn't hurt. He reminded me of Zelda and Zoe, no small accomplishment. Which served to remind me of Lucy and how I obtained Zelda.

I just couldn't win.

Diana was something else. She helped me in Diamondhead while I was tracking down Bobbie the last time the woman disappeared on me. I had to deal with the fact that Diana was a DEA agent—one who'd seen my files. Yes, files. Plural. Why I had two of them, neither of us knew.

Of course, I did some contract work with the DEA. I become emotionally involved with the agent assigned to work with me. Lindy was killed in a firefight on a wharf in Tampico by a double-crossing agent.

I fell in love with Kara, Lindy's replacement. We talked about getting out and making a life together. Then she got pregnant, we got married, and life as I knew it exploded and disappeared in a fireball off Ensenada.

Since all of that, my life was never the same. My second wife, Pilar, also pregnant, was killed in a charter plane crash that occurred when she was flying back to me from a visit to her family. The plane exploded in a fireball.

The government wouldn't do anything about her murderer. They were convinced she was a bomber. I handled it my way. Her killer was eliminated in the most vicious and brutal manner imaginable, thanks to an alligator—my new favorite animal.

Nicolas junior, a killer's son, and Diana, the DEA agent, were involved somehow. Up to their eyeballs. I knew it, but I couldn't prove it. My suspicion was that Nicolas found out how his father died, and took his revenge by killing Andrea.

Informer. Partner. Criminal. Lover. Perhaps Diana could be all the former. Now I was involved with the woman. Wanting to know who Kara's lover was. Who had gotten her pregnant.

DNA testing proved I wasn't the father of Kara's son, James. While that was one load off, who was the father? Was it her DEA supervisor and handler? Was he a contract hire, too, like me? I didn't think so. Notes I read in my file seemed to say otherwise.

What I hadn't done so far was request Kara's DEA file. I wondered if Diana could deliver that up. It would mean I'd have to use her at least one more time. Did I want to do that?

And then, all at once, I had the answer. I had to find out what the hell was going on that my life had become such a tangled, confusing, deadly mess.

Diana would have to come through one more time. I knew what I had to do. She made that plain enough more than once. In the process, I knew she would devour me like a last meal.

My phone pinged, and Maddie knew right off who the text was coming from. She wasn't happy. She knew I was being summoned to view the DEA file on Kara. We talked about it last night in bed, and she agreed to it, but still, if she said no, I wouldn't have listened.

I showed her the text, but even so, Maddie became suddenly quiet and withdrawn. Even Friday was standoffish. Could the darned dog read his moody mistress, or what?

"I won't be long, I promise," I said, not knowing how long I would need to get the information.

"And I won't be waiting up, either. I'm done with that. You're a big boy. You do what you have to. The sooner this is over with, the better for both of us."

Better for us. I took that with me and walked downstairs. Before I realized what was happening, Friday bolted out the door behind me. I reached to hold the door for the dog, waiting for him to go back inside.

"Come on, boy. Go to Maddie."

I made a grab for his collar. Friday dodged and sat down at the curb, just far enough away that I was unable to reach him and hold the door at the same time. I gave up and headed off in the direction of Diana's apartment. I looked back. Friday was still sitting on the sidewalk.

Eventually Maddie would realize her dog wasn't inside and would come down to let him in. I forgot about him and made my way to Diana's, where I rang the buzzer.

Too late, I realized I had company. That darned woman must have given Friday a hand signal I didn't seen. Friday trotted ahead of me through the open door and sat down on the other side of the glass. His expression said smug and satisfied. He wasn't wagging his tail.

"Well, you're such a smartypants, aren't you?

Come on. You can wait outside." I held the door open. The dog refused to budge. "Go find Maddie. Go on."

Friday's head tilted sideways. He looked at me like I was confused. At least, that's the way I took it. I poked the elevator button and waited. The door slid open and Friday bounded in ahead of me once again.

"Damn you, Friday. You take after your mistress. You're a troublemaker, do you know that?"

He woofed softly, seemingly in agreement. The elevator door opened. Before I could take a step, he grabbed the cuff of my pants and wouldn't let go. "Come on, Friday. Be a good boy. I have work to do here."

The dog refused to agree. I gently shook my foot. Friday shook his head, teeth clamped firmly on my pant-leg, refusing to let go.

"Come on, then. You can wait outside her door. If I get close to being in trouble, you can bark, okay?"

Seemingly satisfied, the dog released my foot. He snuffled his way down the corridor as though he knew the way and halted in front of Diana's door. He sat down, off to the side, and waited.

I knocked, and it was like Diana was waiting on the other side. She opened the door almost immediately. "I heard voices. Who were you talking to, Jim?"

I ignored her. The last I saw Friday, he was settling in on the floor against the door. He wasn't looking like he was about to take a doggy snooze.

I spotted the file on the kitchen table and didn't waste time getting to it. Diana stood behind me. She bent and her breasts brushed my neck. They were warm and soft and felt too good. I leaned back, pressing against them.

Distracted, I ended up brushing pages from Kara's file onto the floor. Diana bent to pick them up. I couldn't tear my eyes away, and she knew it.

"I couldn't get all the file," Diana said. "You're going to have to come back for the rest of it."

She pushed herself up on the table and crossed her long, gorgeous legs in front of me. Her robe chose that moment to open, revealing warm, dark nipples that tightened. She sighed and slightly parted her knees. "Come on, Jim. Get comfortable."

It would be too easy. And then I remembered Maddie. I remembered how good she was for me. I didn't want to screw things up any worse than they were with Diana in the middle.

Diana leaned back on the table, daring me to take her. When her feet hooked onto me, I knew I had only seconds before succumbing to charms already too familiar.

In the hall, Friday began barking. "I should chase that dog out of here. He sneaked into the lobby with me and I couldn't get rid of him."

Diana looked like she wanted to hit me. I left her splayed out on the table. If I saw her again, she'd make mincemeat out of me.

"Call me when you get all the file. Not before," I insisted.

"You bastard. I'll—"

I didn't get to hear the rest of it. Friday led me to the staircase and grabbed my leg one more time. The dog pulled me through the door. He must have thought my resolve was weak.

He was right, too. Without him, I would have been putty in Diana's eager hands. Friday made sure to keep me in front of him. It was like he was herding me down the stairs to the lobby.

Happy finally with the results of his stalking, the dog ran back and forth in front of me as we made our way home to his mistress. Still not satisfied, he chased me up the stairs to the small apartment.

"Well now. I see one of you had some common sense. I wondered where he'd gotten to," Maddie said.

"Just how far behind him were you?" I wondered.

"You'll never know. Now come to bed. Your reward is waiting."

I had a feeling I was going to be getting more than a treat and some petting.

Maddie raised her shirt, looked down, and pinched her waist. I figured it wasn't up to me to bring up how much she enjoyed my cooking, so I took the tactful route. "I don't want to hear any complaints about your pants not fitting, woman."

"Judging by the way you keep checking out my ass, I'd say any complaints would fall on deaf ears."

I reached across to join in the pinching. She grinned and made a feeble attempt at slapping my hand away before melting into my arms. "You're spoiling me, Maddie."

She was, too.

"Only because you're a good cook. Can we go back to bed?"

She was a good lover. I wanted to be just as good

for her. "That would be nice, but I have someplace I need to be." Already I knew what was coming.

"Oh, really? Is Diana calling so early in the morning?"

"Yeah. No. I was planning on taking Friday for a walk. Would you like to come with us?"

That appeared to solve it for now, but we both knew it wasn't over. Friday settled into his usual place between us and trotted along. His nose snuffled at our joined hands. For good measure, he gave fingers a lick and seemed content just to be spending time with us.

"When are you going to do the deal with the devil?" Maddie asked.

One thing about Maddie, she had a way with words. "I'll call her later. I may be late getting home tonight."

"I don't want to know. You get home when you get home."

Maddie knew the deal. I didn't bring it up again. If everything went according to plan, I'd never have to see Diana again. For sure, Maddie ought to be pretty happy at that prospect.

I wasn't making any promises, though.

C all display told Diana who was on the other end. "Finally. I was wondering—"

"Wonder no more," I said.

"Are you coming over?"

"I can't right now," I told her. I reminded her about the file I needed.

All of a sudden she didn't sound so happy. Our

next meeting would depend on a file she wasn't supposed to be able to access. She was concerned about getting caught.

"Why don't we meet at my place and talk about it? I could cook you dinner."

My first thought was to turn the invitation down. Without the file, I'd have to go back. Maddie would be furious. I wouldn't be able to keep it from her. At the same time, I had to get eyes on Kara's DEA file, no matter the cost.

"I'll see you at eight," I told her.

I already knew how the woman would work it. She'd tell me she wasn't able to get the file. She'd keep me dangling for a day or two. Maybe as long as a week if she could drag it out. She'd start thinking she had an in with me.

To say Maddie wouldn't be happy would be an understatement. What other option was there? I'd have to make it up to her, or she'd sic Friday on me for sure. Talk about being between a rock and a hard place.

Too late. The minute I walked into the office, Maddie was on me like I'd just come from Diana's bed.

"You're seeing that woman again. I know it. I already know she's not going to turn over that file without a fight. She'll have you hanging on by your fingernails, and I'm not talking about a rock ledge. I'm talking about her back."

I put my hands up in surrender. "All right. I'll call her and cancel. I'll tell her I don't need the file. I'll never see her again for as long as we're together. Is that good enough for you?"

"It's a good start, that's for sure. Let's go upstairs and talk some more about it," Maddie insisted. Even Friday woofed at that offer. Perhaps I should have, too.

"I can't. She invited me for dinner."

Maddie's hands went to her hips. Suddenly, I felt like a very bad boy.

"Who's cooking?" Why would she want to know that?

"She is."

"Can she cook?"

"How the hell would I know? I've never spent that much time with her."

"Yeah, well, if you know what's good for you, you won't be making her breakfast in the morning. You'll be here making it for me and Friday. And that's final."

"Will I get to keep Friday if you leave?" It was my way of trying to keep it light. It didn't go over well.

"I'm smart enough to know that if I leave it up to Friday to make the decision, the answer will be no."

That was good enough.

12

I already knew I was treading on hazardous ground with another visit to Diana. Maddie had every right to be angry. Even Friday was giving me the cold shoulder. When I offered to take him for a walk, he shuffled away, head hanging and tail stilled, in search of his mistress. For sure I was in the doghouse when Friday didn't want to associate with me.

Maddie made it clear she didn't want me having anything more to do with Diana. I clung to the excuse that I needed to see Kara's DEA file. Diana was the only person who could get it, I explained. It wasn't an excuse so much as the truth.

Without that file, I'd be no further ahead.

Wanting to occupy some time, I wheeled Maddie's chair to her desk and began going through the drawers. The hidden kitty money I let her use until the first paycheck was replaced. A bottom drawer held treats and a couple of toys for Friday. I squeezed a rubber bone. The desultory squeak didn't summon the dog.

At the back of another drawer, my hand touched something that shouldn't be there. An old burn phone. I flipped it open. The battery needed charging. I put it back in the drawer and yelled up the stairs. "Want to share some takeout? I'm going to order Chinese."

No answer. Not even from Friday. I ordered anyway and headed up to the apartment. I scrubbed the kitchen sink, put out a tablecloth, and dug around for some candles.

you're invited over for dinner

it's not dinnertime i have things to do

it's dinnertime somewhere in the world how about it???

what did you get for Friday

Aha. She was all about using the dog ploy. Friday was now as much a part of my life as Maddie.

send him over and I'll show you

Friday pranced through the open door into the kitchen. The dog's tail wagged furiously. He plopped down and looked up at me with a huge doggy grin. At least, it seemed like a grin, since I was the one in the doghouse. Any bit of attention would do.

I scratched behind his ears. Slipped him a treat. Tied a bandanna around his neck. Held out a card. He took it in his mouth and scampered off in Maddie's direction, tail still wagging furiously. It seemed like forever until he returned, mouth empty.

"Good boy, Friday."

It took Maddie even longer.

The dog plopped down on his haunches beside me, and we waited. The nervous waiting was worth every minute. Maddie was stunning in the sleek little black dress. She turned to show off the back. It was cut just as low as the front. My eyes barely left the inviting curve of her breasts, plainly visible from front and side.

"You look fantastic. Come over here."

She looked doubtful, as though she needed convincing. "I'm not coming over there for you just to mess everything up. Is the food here?" she asked.

"Not yet. We have time."

Friday seemed to think so, too, by the way he was looking from one to the other. The buzzer sounded, and suddenly we didn't.

I lit the candles and dimmed the lights. If Maddie was trying to teach me a lesson, she succeeded. By the end of the meal, I was ready for the dessert she was teasing me with throughout.

Maddie finished and slipped off in a sweaty, hot mess of tangled arms and legs and damp bodies on sticky sheets. "I can't any more, Jim. It's too much."

"That's good. I can't either."

She collapsed beside me while I traced patterns down her damp back and lower. Goosebumps teased my fingertips. "Well maybe I can. Do you want to try?"

A hand reached for me. "Oh. It feels like you can,

too."

We finished together, heaving, crying out, thrusting, each taking from the other what we wanted.

"I can't move off of you. I'm too tired."

"Then don't. Stay right there."

She uncrossed her ankles and slipped her feet down the bed. Somehow, the motion kept me in her, still hard. "Oh my goodness. Jim. We're making love," she said.

She brought her knees up and that wasn't all we ended up doing. When we were truly finished, I pulled the sheet up and we nodded off in each other's arms.

I woke and made my way to the shower alone. Maddie was waiting when I came out, eager and needy and wanting. "If you're going to her place, you're going so damned tired you won't be able to spit," she insisted.

Maddie was right about that. It was all I could do to manage a dry swallow as I walked down the stairs. I stopped at the office and flipped open the phone I left behind on charge.

Maddie yelled down the stairs. "Should I wait up for you? I want to be able to stab you from the front. No surprises."

I called back. "Don't forget you own a gun, too."

Like I needed to remind her. There was nothing on the phone. It wasn't on charge long enough. The phone ended up on the desk.

I climbed up the stairs. My arms circled the

woman and held her tight. "Wait up for me. I won't be long."

A squeeze and a pat later, and I headed for the door. It was all I could do to keep my eyes open. I even went so far as to think about pulling the car over and slipping into the back seat for a quick nap.

If Maddie wasn't waiting, I might have, too. My guilty mind wandered to the phone in the office and the waiting text messages. Bobbie. Who else could it be? Andrea? Maybe, perhaps with a sent text as a clue before she was murdered. Could I get that lucky?

I pulled up in front of Diana's and forgot about the phone and the messages it might contain. I had other things occupying my mind.

First among them was how to get the information I needed before slipping away from Diana's clutches. Having Maddie not kill me when I got home would be a bonus.

I turned down the after-dinner drink Diana offered. She insisted on making coffee. She left the room and I rested my head on the back of the sofa. In seconds my eyes closed and I was gone, exhausted, overtaken by sleep.

An impatient woman gave me a shove and I woke up. Groggy and unsure of where I was, my eyes opened just as Diana's robe conveniently chose that moment to part. A well-formed and dark-tipped breast waved. She made no attempt to cover it. When it didn't have the reaction she wanted, she shook me again.

"What? What is it?"

I stretched. The back of my fingers brushed a warm breast. Her nipple tightened and I knew I had to get out. Diana stood and allowed the rest of her robe to open. Beneath it she was completely naked.

"You could barely keep your eyes open all during dinner," she said. "Why are you so tired? You sat down beside me and fell asleep almost immediately."

She opened the robe wide, putting her need on display. My eyes weakened and wandered for a last look before she closed up shop. Trying to torture me. It wasn't working.

"It's been a long day. I spent most of it in a hot car on a stakeout."

I wanted the lie to work. The thin robe and Diana's dark, erect nipples were working to weaken my already flimsy resolve.

"I didn't let you come here to sleep," she said.

Yeah, I knew all about that, all right. "Did you get the file?" It was time to get down to business.

She didn't mention it during dinner, and I didn't ask. No need to make it obvious why I was really there.

"Not yet. You're going to have to come back."

Like I didn't see that coming a mile away. "I have to get to bed. I can barely keep my eyes open."

"You're not sleeping here. I want a wide-awake man," she said.

So my ruse was working after all. Her hands shook and fumbled with the tie on her robe, wanting me to be witness to her need once more. Suddenly she swept it closed, resolved that she wouldn't be getting what she so obviously wanted. "Did you see what's waiting for you? Now get out."

I saw, all right. I rubbed at my eyes. "You're right. I'd be no good for either of us. Call me when you get the file."

I barely made a successful escape. Even so, proud of my unbroken resolve, I whistled tunelessly while making for the car. I'm not so sure why whistling came to mind. I couldn't whistle worth a damn.

All the way home I thought of Maddie and even Friday and wondered if they'd be waiting. They couldn't possibly run off the way Bobbie had, could they?

I opened the door to the building to see Maddie sitting at the top of the stairs. Friday was plunked down beside her. She was petting him absentmindedly. I figured it was Maddie's way of making sure I didn't sneak into bed beside her without getting the third degree because she was asleep.

"You're back late."

Maddie couldn't bring herself to look at me. Instead, she hugged Friday closer. He rewarded her by licking her cheek. "How did it go with Diana?"

It was like a lightbulb going off when I realized she was worried about that woman getting into my life.

"You know, you could scratch me like that and see what happens," I said, smiling.

"Well then, get your ass up here. I did laundry. The bed's fresh-made. All I need to know is if you deserve it. And me."

"What about Friday?" I wanted to know.

"He can make up his own mind. Just like you."

Maddie had a mischievous look about her. "Come on, Friday, your master is home. Let's see if your mistress can get a rise out of him. If she can't, we'll just wait until he falls asleep and—"

Maddie didn't finish, but she was grinning. I wasn't worried. She made a grab and pulled me into the bedroom. The image of Diana's wide-open robe disappeared, to be replaced by Maddie's urgent hips rising to follow mine on the way to a successful, hurried release for both of us.

I died and went to heaven, encouraged by Maddie's eager cooing. She finished with me and sat up. She didn't bother to drag the sheet up. We were too familiar with each other for that. "Nash, if this is what sending you to that woman does, go more often, would you?"

I barely heard her. I was that close to sleep. Maybe if I mumbled. "I have to go back."

I wasn't so sleepy that I knew that wouldn't work before the words came out. It was about to hit the fan, and I was too tired to care.

"What?" Maddie rolled away from me. As far as she could get without ending up on the floor.

I couldn't lie. "She didn't have the file."

"She's playing you."

"Probably. But are you happy with how?"

I pulled her close beneath the sheets, a body nice and warm and familiar. She could refuse, but she didn't. Her body melted against mine.

"Yes. I'm not happy to hear you have to go back, though. I'm going to have to do something about that."

I fell deep into dreamless sleep. I didn't hear a word.

We spent a leisurely breakfast in bed. My mind was on downstairs and the office of Dawson and Nash. The burner phone I left behind. We played in the shower until I couldn't wait any longer. Maddie looked at me quizzically.

"The phone," I reminded her. "I let it charge overnight."

I hurried to dress and rushed downstairs in hot pursuit of the waiting texts I knew would be there. I halted on the landing. What if there were no texts from the woman? What if Bobbie left me for real?

The journey became a lot longer. My steps slowed and almost stopped. I halted at the office door, the handle almost burning my hand as I twisted it open. There it was, on the desk where I left it. I rushed to flip the old phone open.

Nothing. No light. No charge.

It was plugged in. I wiggled the cable. I checked the outlet. Still nothing.

Shit.

I sat down at the desk. I flung open drawers and rummaged frantically. Not a damned one. Where the hell was the proper cable? I yelled up the stairs in a panic. "Maddie?"

Her head poked out from the stairwell. "What? What's wrong?" She hesitated at the top of the stairs.

"It's the wrong cable. The phone won't charge."

It was an old flip. There was no SIM. There was nothing to put into a modern phone. I switched power outlets. Still nothing. By then, Maddie was on her way downstairs, waving a tangled cord in her hand. "This has to be it."

"Where did you find it?"

"I forgot I left it in my bag."

I grabbed the cable and plugged in the phone. "We should know in a few minutes. Let's take a walk and stop for coffee."

We headed off to a tiny bistro a block away and took a table on the sidewalk. Under normal circumstances, it would be halfway romantic, but the phone wouldn't leave my thoughts.

"Are you sure that was the cable?"

"I'm sure. If I remember right, it was wrapped around the phone when I found it," she said.

We were too distracted to take the time for a leisurely coffee. I paid the barista to pour it into a couple of go-cups and we rushed back to the office. It was only half a block before we trashed the coffee.

By the time we made the office we were practically running. Friday looked up from his bed in the office and woofed. Even he was surprised to see us so soon.

"Double shit." There was no light on the phone's face. There it was. Plain as day in the display. *Battery Bad*. I flipped the phone open, hoping.

"Dammit to hell. We need to find a replacement battery."

My own phone rang. I looked to see who it was and slipped it back into my pocket. I wasn't fast enough.

"Who was it?" she asked.

I called to Friday. He waddled over and sat beside me, looking anxious. I scratched him behind his ears and he sighed.

"Don't be dragging my dog into this. It was Diana, wasn't it?"

The dog's ears pricked up at hearing the woman's name. Maddie was probably talking to him about her. Even the dog had the good sense to desert me and go sit beside his mistress.

There was no point in lying. "Yes."

"Call her back."

She led Friday upstairs. His tail stayed visible, sticking past the corner, thumping up and down. I guessed Maddie was with him. Eavesdropping. Fine by me.

"You can both hear better from down here," I called after them. Friday settled in at Maddie's feet, in front of the sofa. The dog really did desert me.

"So make the call already, Nash."

Friday's tail didn't wag once while I was on the phone. By the same token, Maddie didn't look so happy, either.

I finally found a compatible battery and swapped it out. Finally, I could read the texts.

"They're all from Bobbie. Quite a few, too."

I looked at the dates. They were days old. I checked the calendar. The texts started the day she left. Why hadn't she said anything to me? Why did she sneak off the way she did?

Absentmindedly, I scratched at Friday. Somehow, I found it comforting.

i'm with Nicolas. i have to know if he did it. i can't

delay any longer

I finally knew why Bobbie left without a word. I would have tried to talk her out of it. Bobbie knew it, too. That's why she packed her bag and ran off after dispatching me for food.

We were devastated when Andrea was killed, although it affected Bobbie much more than it did me. Andrea only just finished the amazing office painting. She set up the computer and the office video recording system. Bobbie and I talked about making her a partner in the business, and she was well on her way to earning a full partnership.

What I didn't tell Bobbie was that I hadn't turned on the surveillance system. We had no video of the murder in our own office. A broken neck. It wasn't from a fall, although the ladder was tipped to make it look like it. Someone wrapped their hands around her throat while standing in front of her. Bobbie was convinced it was Nicolas.

i'm at nick's place in the everglades. it's going to plan. i managed to worm my way in. don't ask. please.

Shit. The texts were days old. Bobbie was partnered up with Nicolas. He was her suspect in Andrea's murder. Perhaps the man found out his father became feed for the alligators and we did nothing to stop it. That the old man was intent on killing us at the time wouldn't matter in the slightest. The son was no doubt intent on avenging his father's death.

It didn't take Nicholas long to put two and two

together. I wondered if he was planning the same for Bobbie. And eventually, me.

i have Andrea's gun. i'm safe

She was safe so far. I checked the date again. Days ago still. Damn it. Why didn't I listen to Maddie the first time she showed me the phone? And then she had to remind me.

"I tried telling you. You wouldn't let me. I tucked it back in the drawer where I found it."

Maddie was right. We were headed out on our first stakeout together. She started digging around in her bag. For some reason it annoyed me. She held up the phone like a prize and I as much as ignored her. Shit.

"It's not your fault. I'm the one that shut you down."

Maddie's pale face said she felt responsible. I held out my hand to reassure her. She took it and squeezed hard. "I should have spoken up."

I drew her to me and my arms went around her. "You couldn't have known. It was your first day. We were getting to know each other. You didn't want to piss off your boss on your first job out of the office. We have to figure out what we're going to do about it."

"Do you think Diana has any part in it?" she asked.

"I don't know. Nick and Diana look to me to be pretty tight. You saw them, too. Meeting. Talking. Something is going on for sure."

"Could she be dirty?" Maddie asked.

Damn. I never once thought that about the woman. I wondered if Maddie was only bringing it up because she was jealous that I was seeing her.

"Your guess would be as good as mine. I don't know if we have enough time to find out."

I scrolled down to the end of the texts.

are you getting these?

Then hours later.

where are you, Jim?

The texts halted. There were no others. I punched in a reply and hoped she hadn't given up. The reply came immediately.

where have you been

I looked across at Maddie.

there's too much to explain want to do it in person

you can't. not now too soon. he finally started trusting me. talk tomorrow

Would Bobbie call? Or would it be another text?

"She's all right, Maddie. Whatever it is she's doing, it's working." Maybe she thought so. I wasn't convinced. Neither was Maddie.

"Is she undercover?"

"I guess. But don't ask me more than that. I don't know. I'm starting to wonder if you might be right."

"How so?"

"That Nicolas and Diana are working together somehow. That the woman is dirty."

"How are we going to find out?" Maddie asked.

"I have no idea."

"You're going to have to see her again," she said.

She seemed to have forgotten I'd be seeing her anyway. Diana still didn't have the file on Kara I needed to see.

"Are you all right with that?"

"I guess I'm going to have to be, aren't I?"

I looked at the phone again. There was nothing from Bobbie for a day. Then this.

i think he's on to me

It was the last text Bobbie sent.

13

It wasn't as difficult as Bobbie Dawson thought it would be. She sent Nash off for the all too familiar coffee and burritos they liked. In his absence, she cleaned up with a quick shower. Threw some things in a bag. Took a last look around before closing the door behind her.

She made Nick promise not to park in front of the building. The last thing she needed was Jim recognizing the hothead. A street brawl would surely follow. She exited the building with every sense alert. A horn honked and echoed off the buildings. She recognized the convertible parked in the next block.

Andrea's death was the cause of all the subterfuge. Something about it bothered her. That something wouldn't let up. That's the reason she was leaving Jim. It wasn't that Andrea was murdered in the office. Yet, it had to be more than a robbery gone wrong. There was nothing missing. That Andrea had been strangled face-to-face told her whoever it was wanted Andrea to know who did it. Wanted to watch her suffer.

Even with that, she had nothing definite to go on.

It was more of a gut feeling. That feeling told her to keep an eye on Nick, the son of the man she and Jim allowed an alligator to snack on. That Nicolas senior had been holding a gun to their heads didn't make it a hard decision.

It wasn't easy to be leaving with Nick, but she had at least some of it covered. She tossed the old burner phone into her desk. When Jim was bored, he had a habit of going through all the drawers in the office. He'd find the phone and get the texts she planned on sending.

When her first morning with Nick came around, she got a clue there was something wrong with that thesis. Jim never responded to her texts. By the end of day two, she was desperate. Nicolas was pressing her to share his bed. Why wouldn't he? She'd used every trick in her book to get to him. She was hard pressed to push him away.

Nick wouldn't be kept at bay forever.

Bobbie hadn't counted on Nicolas being a total turnoff. Nothing about the man was likable in the slightest. Not that she was looking for romance, but a little wouldn't have hurt. He reeked of B.O. Every shirt he put on was wrinkled. Like he let them sit in the dryer until he needed one to wear.

When she had no response to her texts from Jim over the following days, she took up with Ron, one of the boat captains, on the sly. And why not? It took the edge off and it was convenient when Nick disappeared into the swamp as he did from time to time.

It meant she got a lot of sunshine. Nick didn't seem to notice, and she was grateful for the break in the sexual monotony. Neither of her lovers were as good as Jim. Which she guessed was her way of making herself feel only a little guilty.

On the other hand, she was getting a nice tan. Jim would no doubt have fun exploring whenever she got herself out of this hell-hole. If she got out. She was beginning to wonder.

When would Jim find the phone and investigate the texts?

"I've got to do a test run, Bobbie. Want to come along?" Ron asked.

His request distracted her. She looked forward to these escapes from reality with an eager stranger. She found she was no less eager. The instant they were out of sight beyond the promontory, she slipped off her bikini bottom beneath the sarong. She unzipped the driver and they were in the wind. There was something about wind at her back while she engaged in enthusiastic sex with a man she hardly knew.

There was something about being naked in the watery wilderness with a turned-on man in a swamp infested with alligators, too. It took her over the edge. She always returned sated. She always returned eager for the next time.

Face flushed, sweaty in places she shouldn't be, and bearing bruises courtesy of the boat captain's unbridled enthusiasm, she returned happy and refreshed. It was always a rush to adjust clothing to cover places that were naked only minutes before docking.

Yet she wasn't truly happy. She left Jim behind,

alone and unsupported. Somehow, she'd make it up to him. She had to. She sent off another text, completely dejected that he hadn't responded to any of them. Perhaps that sense of rejection was the reason for her heightened sexuality.

It was while Bobbie was out on a test drive with Ron, the boat captain. Ron was the one to bring up Diana's name. Ron took Diana out into the swamp, too. The woman was still involved with Nicolas somehow. Bobbie wondered if Diana's tan was coming along as nicely as hers.

According to Ron, their meetings were all talk and no sex, something she thought unusual. The last time she saw Diana, the woman's legs were pointing at the roof and Nicolas was happily ensconced between them, grunting in happy release.

So what were they doing out in the swamp? Meeting someone else? Hauling drugs? Feeding alligators with fresh bodies?

She cooed into Nick's ear on a nightly basis. Hell, she cooed into his ear during the day too, hoping he might be better in bed in the afternoon. To no avail. If Jim ever found out she was sleeping with two men—but then, she couldn't exactly say she was getting any sleep, could she?

Damn but she wanted this to be over. She was starting to regret the guilty feelings overtaking her. Then, just when she thought Jim deserted her, he responded to her texts. They must have gone through all at once.

He thought she deserted him. If only he knew

what she was up to. He'd be appalled. She was feeling guilty enough already.

That Bobbie took it upon herself to prove Nicolas was the guilty party in Andrea's murder didn't sit well. Why hadn't the woman said something? Having finally discovered her texts, I had to get out to the swamp and see for myself.

I found Maddie's keys, intending to take her car without asking. That I managed a pair of camo pants and a dark tee without her noticing was a miracle in itself. If it wasn't for those damned texts—

I agonized over whether I should do it at all. Bobbie was an adult. She knew what she'd be letting herself in for. And I knew if she was with Nick, she'd be sleeping with him. How else would it work?

The last drive I took to the everglades had Andrea sitting beside me. We'd developed an easy rapport since I'd hired her. Even Bobbie liked her. With her qualifications, the woman was well on her way to a full partnership in the business.

So much for all that. Andrea was gone now, and her loss had affected Bobbie deeply. She took it personal, and that had to be why she traipsed off to Nick's place in the everglades. She had to have a reason to suspect him as Andrea's murderer.

What that could be—

The police investigated and came up with nothing. Whoever was responsible was long gone. No robbery motive. All her things were left behind. Andrea was in the process of setting up the video system after painting the picture for us.

It was close to twilight when I turned onto the side road. I kept my lights off and slowly made my way on the dirt road to search for somewhere to park and not be seen.

Maddie's short wheelbase rocked and rolled its way down an unfamiliar, overgrown trail. Before the light failed completely I turned around, not wanting to get stuck in the swampy grounds. Satisfied, I walked to the gravel road and made my way to the buildings in the darkness.

It was day's end and the business was in shutdown. Someone started a party in front of one of the trailers beside the wharf. Lights and loud music and a smoking barbecue put everyone in party mode, probably a staple of life in the humid, smelly swamp.

Bobbie ambled into view on the way to the party. She carried a beer. She finished it and threw it into a box before moving to dance with a male in the small crowd. Her hips undulated beneath the sarong. Her breasts shook in the tiny bikini top.

She appeared to be enjoying herself until Nicolas approached. She pushed away and danced to a seat at a picnic table covered in bottles. She leaned back and crossed her legs beneath the sarong. It parted to reveal familiar long legs.

Nicolas sat beside her and kissed her neck. He whispered something in her ear. She squirmed and finally relented to let him nuzzle her. She got up and headed for the chickee with hips swaying in a seductive, come-hither motion.

She disappeared into the back of the house. Nick followed not far behind. I already knew where the bedrooms were from my last visit. In minutes, Nick made his way back to the music and the party.

I saw enough. Bobbie was safe, at least. Our relationship, not so much from what I witnessed. I called it a night went to head back to the car.

"Jim." A familiar voice and a hand on my shoulder forced me to halt mid-step. "What are you doing here?"

"I needed to know you were safe, Bobbie. It was the only way since you stopped answering texts."

"I didn't get any. I thought you gave up on me."

She was out in the boonies. Maybe it was reception. Or a lack of it.

"In that case, you've got a bunch waiting. I couldn't wait any longer. I couldn't stop with the worrying. I had to see you."

"I'm all right," Bobbie said. "I'm getting closer to finding out if he killed Andrea."

"Yeah. I noticed that right off."

"What do you expect? That I'd be out here and be a virgin? You know as well as anyone how it works."

That was true. Since Bobbie left, I was already in a relationship of some sort with a woman who was supposed to be a secretary. Too soon was she turning into another live-in partner.

"I know how it goes. How close are you?" I wanted to know. Hell, I was jealous as hell. I needed to know. She ignored the question.

"I think Diana is hooked into this thing, too. She comes out here occasionally. Not on a regular basis. They have meetings. Don't ask me what about. I don't know. They go out in one of the boats and they don't include me. For all I know he's screwing her out there."

Now who was jealous? And jealous of the man she was investigating, to boot. Life wasn't fair.

"I miss you. I want you safe. If he did murder Andrea, you're not safe out here in the boonies. Hell, you can't even get a simple text."

"Did it have hearts?"

I reached around and pinched her rear. It got a giggle before she pushed my hand away and went all serious. "Don't. You know how I feel about you. You're going to force me out of character if you're not careful." She didn't know I'd seen Nick follow her to the bedroom.

"All right. I'm going. Be careful. Be safe. If you're not going to come with me, at least get your ass back to where you're safe. I don't want you getting hurt."

Without another word I turned and walked to the car. I stopped in the darkness before pulling out onto the gravel road. I looked across at the party in full swing beneath the lights. Bobbie was up on a table, swinging her hips to the rhythm of the music. Nick stared up at her. She stared down at another man who looked back at her with a huge grin pasted on his face. Who the hell was that?

Disappointed. Empty-handed. I carried on home, worrying all the way. It wasn't only Bobbie's safety that concerned me. It was the well-being of our relationship, too.

14

I **wasn't exactly overjoyed** to learn Bobbie was living in a swamp with the son of the man we had allowed to become alligator food. The positive was that she was alive and well. I was happy knowing she hadn't deserted me, even if she was shacked up with Nicolas.

How Maddie would take it when I broke the news my business partner and lover hadn't deserted me, I had no idea. I knew I couldn't live with myself if I didn't spill.

For sure Maddie knew something was up the instant I walked in the door. Even Friday made sure to keep his distance. Before I had a chance to open my mouth, Maddie got out the candles and eased me into a chair. "We need to talk."

That wasn't a lie. Ever one for grandstanding, Friday plopped down at my feet and looked up with a baleful expression. If I knew what was good for everyone involved, I wouldn't shut up until I finished.

"I found Bobbie." Blurted wouldn't be a word I'd ordinarily use. Even so, I halted right there.

Maddie stopped what she was doing, sat in my lap, and waited. She wasn't going to be about making it easy. Unlike Friday, her expression wasn't baleful. I wasn't sure how to characterize it.

"I took a drive out to the everglades to the site of an old case of ours. Andrea was in on that one, too."

"Don't stop now if you know what's good for you," Maddie said.

My hand wandered to the small of her back. It didn't fool her.

"Shamus, if I was going to shoot you, I would have done it when you told me about your involvement with Diana. I accepted it as part of the job, didn't I?"

So much for being surreptitious. And shamus was a new one, not used for decades.

"Now tell me what's going on. I want to be able to make my own decisions."

I filled her in on what I discovered at Nick's tour business. She wasn't unhappy to know Bobbie was alive and well. "You did your job. You checked on your partner once you figured out where she was. Now you know. We know. You're relieved, and so am I. I knew you were wondering what was going on with her. You needed to find out."

So then why was I so concerned about Maddie? Bobbie was safe and sound. She wasn't back in my life yet, but I was certain she would be at some point. Besides, she was my business partner, too.

"Maddie—"

She pressed a finger to my lips. "Shh. I'm here. You're here. We've been good together so far. Let's not spoil it until we can't go any longer, okay? Deal?"

I kissed her slowly. She melted into me. Before I knew it we were in the bedroom and the dinner she so lovingly prepared was going cold.

So was Friday. We closed the bedroom door on him. We weren't about coming out until we had it settled between us. We didn't come out then, either.

We made love again.

T he explosion shook the building. Windows shattered. We rushed to look down on what was left of a burning car. Licks of orange flame pushed thick, black smoke skyward. The odor of gasoline and rubber and plastic drifted into the building.

"That's my car!" Maddie exclaimed.

"Are you sure? Is that where you usually park?" I knew it was. Someone was sending a message, and they weren't going to be satisfied until I got it. "Maddie. Listen to me." I took her face in my hands. Her whole body was shaking. "You can't ever walk out of this place unarmed. In fact, I want you armed all the time now. Someone isn't happy with us."

Talk about minimizing an obvious threat. It was an understatement.

"Do you think Bobbie had anything to do with it?" she asked.

Flashing lights illuminated buildings. Sirens screamed.

"She couldn't have. I didn't have time to tell her about you." That was true. All Bobbie wanted to do after warning me off was to get back to the party.

"But Nick could have told her. If Diana mentioned me. Maybe he'd want Bobbie to know to cement his relationship with her."

Damn it, this woman was good. I would never have thought of it that way. "You could be right. All the more reason for you to be armed. I think you know I don't want to lose you. Or your friend out in the hall."

"Oh come on. You know darned well you'd use any excuse to steal Friday," she said.

"Not unless you're a part of the deal, woman. Know it and weep."

"I think Bobbie might have something to say about that, shamus. Even I don't think you're dumb enough to believe it."

She was right. We both knew it. "Maddie—"

"Don't say it, and I won't say it."

"Maddie—"

"No, Jim. Don't. We can't. Not now."

She left me with a measure of hope, at least. Or was she saying not now that we knew what Bobbie was up to in that damned swamp?

Maddie's bombed-out car said someone was out to scare us off. But who? Nicolas? Had Bobbie told him I'd been out to visit her? Pillow talk, perhaps.

That meant her relationship with Nicolas was more than she let on. But surely that was impossible. Bobbie was out to learn who killed Andrea. Would she tell someone she suspected of murder that I'd been to see her? That would blow her cover all to hell.

Of course, she could have told him I figured out where she was. That I came to try to win her back.

That would light a fire under Nick. Maybe it would have encouraged him to send me a message. To send a message about Maddie.

If Nick saw it as messing with Bobbie, he would use it as an excuse to damn well mess with Maddie.

Diana knew about Maddie, of course. She couldn't know we were sleeping together, although she let it be known that she suspected. But why would she be jealous of Maddie? She had no reason. Did she think there was a chance of a relationship with me beyond the files she had access to? The file I wanted on Kara?

Surely not. Although the sex was good, I didn't trust Diana as far as I could throw her.

It had to be someone else. Something else. I'd give my last dollar to find out who or what.

15

We **were into it** now. Up to our collective necks and the swamp was gaining, thanks to Bobbie. She ran off alone. She had done it in the past. Hadn't said word one. I was supposed to know by osmosis that she was off kicking ass and solving crime.

Her problem now was one that I had no control over. In the past, I'd been there for her. More than once, I'd rescued her because of her refusal to include me in her plans.

Hell, the very first time I saw her, I dropped everything and came to her rescue. Gas station hoodlums attempting to make her their own when they tried loading her into a half-ton. That her problem then became mine had no bearing on my situation. I volunteered to abandon everything in order to help find her brother.

Now the woman had run off on another one of her schemes in an ill-advised attempt to right a wrong and solve a murder. That it was in the middle of a swamp infested with alligators didn't phase her in the slightest. There were enough gators in the swamp. She didn't need a two-legged one in her life. That I made a decision to turn Andrea's murder over to Detective Boyle in the local PD had no effect on the woman. I recognized I was too close to it. Why couldn't Bobbie?

She would have to make short work of Nicolas, or give it up entirely for her safety. The only problem? She didn't know it. Or she was ignoring the obvious.

It would be difficult if not impossible for me to come to her rescue again. By the time she got word out, she could already be on her way to being fresh meat in an alligator-infested swamp.

Maddie became a nervous wreck following her car's destruction. She wasn't cut out for what I got her involved in. She was in over her head, too. The good thing was, she didn't try to deny it, unlike Bobbie.

"We'll get you a new car first thing, sweetheart."

She looked at me in disbelief. "I can't afford a new car. I could barely afford the old one."

"You found your sugar daddy, baby. I'm all cars for you." I tried keeping it light. The humor wasn't appreciated.

"How am I going to pay for it on what you pay me? Explain to me that, Mr. Detective man."

"Come back to bed and I'll show you."

"Show me?" She gathered her robe and closed it, leaving it unfastened. So there was some hope after all.

"Show me what, exactly? I've already seen everything you've got to offer. I might add that I like what I see."

She halted for effect. "So far."

The robe fell open. "In that case, you ain't seen

nuttin' yet. There's a new car in that bedroom. There might even be one on the sofa in the living room if you're good."

Maddie picked out a little convertible number. Bright yellow. Alloy rims. Loaded for bear with all the goodies. I felt good paying for it, too. How could I not? I was the reason her car was destroyed.

"Man, I'm going to be stylin' it when I have to pack up and move back into my car," she said.

My stomach dropped out. I didn't so much as take a breath. It never occurred to me she might want a van. It also never occurred to me she might ever want to move out. Which is why I suddenly had a stomach problem. "We could look at vans."

She grinned. "Yeah. No. I wouldn't know what to do with all the room. Unless you wanted to come with me."

That was easy. "Promise me you'll keep the car locked with the alarm on."

"I promise. Now let's go for a drive." She took us out on the highway. It didn't take a detective to realize we were on the way to Nick's swamp boat business.

"Maddie. Do you think this is a good idea?" I asked.

We were turning off onto the gravel road and I sure as hell wasn't convinced.

"I want him to know I won't be intimidated by his nonsense," she said.

There was no stopping the woman. She was as strong-willed as any woman I'd ever had in my life. As strong-willed as all of them put together.

The thing is, I feared it was going to be a problem real soon now.

Maddie didn't halt in the gravel parking lot. She drove up to the dock and braked in a cloud of dust. I caught sight of Bobbie out on the wharf with what looked to be one of the boat captains.

They were in conversation. Her hand on his arm. Looking up at him. They were about to embrace until our arrival interrupted them. She recognized me immediately. She separated herself in a hurry and made for the car

Maddie was all questions. "Is that her? Where's her boyfriend? Who's she with? Is that Nick? That's not Nick."

Bobbie halted. Looked suddenly uncertain. I'd never seen her in such an agitated state. "Jim? Who's this?"

Well shit. Here we go. Unstoppable object, meet immovable force. I made the introductions quickly. Bobbie looked around. Nervous. Cat-like.

"Nick isn't here. You shouldn't be, either, Nash. What are you doing here with this woman? Who is she?" Bobbie asked.

"She's the woman I hired to replace you. You ran off and didn't tell me, remember? I checked the closet. Your clothes were gone. Nothing left behind. What was I supposed to think?"

"You never told me about her the last time you were here."

"You didn't give me a chance, remember? You were in too much of a hurry to get back to the party," I reminded her.

"You saw."

"Of course I saw. Do you think I'm stupid? Two men, Bobbie? At the same time?"

Maddie was saving her words up to now. "What the hell are you doing out here? You run off, not saying a word. You think you're a special little snowflake, one that doesn't understand consequences. Jim thought you left him. That's why I'm here. Don't you get it?"

Maddie opened the car door. "Come on, Jim. I don't think this woman is worth your time or the trouble she's getting you into."

I was starting to wonder. Maddie could be right.

"And tell your little boyfriend number two—or is he number three—that I'll own him for blowing up my car if it takes forever."

Bobbie looked stunned. "What? What car? What happened?"

Maddie didn't give her the dignity of a response. She punched the accelerator. Bobbie was enveloped in a cloud of dust and dirt thanks to tires set spinning by Maddie's heavy foot. She halted before pulling onto the highway.

"She didn't know about the car. It was pretty plain by the shocked look on her face," I said.

"Very good, detective. Is there anything else you want to tell me?"

I ignored the question and looked out the window. I had a suspicion I'd be doing that a lot with this one. "Who was that man on the dock she was with?"

Maddie's voice had a hard edge. I had to tell her I didn't know.

"She's sleeping with him."

There went my day.

It was a long drive to the office. Maddie tried to cheer me up. Her last resort was putting the top down on her brand-new convertible and allowing me to take over the driver's seat. That didn't work either.

"You'll figure something out. I think you're the kind of person who always does," she said.

Was it a vote of confidence, or was she only trying to cheer me up? Whatever, it was working, finally. I was in a pretty good mood by the time I pulled up in front of the office. I made sure to send a text to Diane to let her know I'd be over later.

"Friday is going to need a walk. We should take him. Give me a minute, okay?" Maddie bounded up the stairs. She returned in a filmy little number that swished with every step.

"You know how to impress a guy. Even Friday is looking at you."

"Are you telling me I'm going to the dogs?"

We burst out laughing.

"No. I'm telling you that when we get back from the walk, you're in big trouble. Maybe even office desk trouble. Come on, Friday. Your mistress and I need to get back in a hurry for an appointment."

Maddie pushed me out the door. Poor Friday was only confused.

It wasn't soon enough for Bobbie to be out of my thoughts just yet, but Maddie was working on it. Maybe what we were doing was right after all.

<h1 style="text-align:center">16</h1>

It was over. Finally. It was over with Bobbie. She had Nick as a lover. By the look of it, she might even have two lovers. It was the final straw. Situation resolved. I was only too happy that it would be Maddie and Friday in my life now. I was glad to have them. Happy about it, even.

We moved into a new phase in our relationship. It was one where I made sure she was safe. If she went out, I made sure Friday went with her. I made sure she was carrying. I made sure she accompanied me to the gun range for training. After a word with Harry, the owner and former cop, he made sure to put her through the paces every time she showed up.

I still had a job to do. It still involved Diana. It would involve her until I could get a look at Kara's old DEA file. But would the file reveal new information?

Together with Maddie's help, I continued to shadow Nick and Diana's comings and goings in the city. Nick seemed to show up randomly. He met Diana in a bar. Heads bent. Deep in conversation. I was never able to eavesdrop.

They had to know I was chasing them. They never once acknowledged it. It was like I didn't exist. It was the same for Maddie. I wasn't sure if it was because Diana was jealous, or if the woman gave up on us.

My phone pinged. A text from Diana. I didn't open it. I figured she was all about rubbing my nose in the fact that I was tailing her and she wasn't about caring.

Maddie was at my desk. She was busy rummaging through the drawers as she usually did when she was bored. Her hand came up with an envelope. "What's this? It's sealed."

Shit. Boyle dropped it off earlier. I forgot all about it. "Boyle."

"Your cop buddy. What's in it?" she asked.

"I didn't open it."

"Kinda like what you do with burn phones. Do you think it might be important in the slightest, Nash?" Her eyes moved to the sign in the window. "You do advertise a detective agency."

I sighed. It seemed like Friday sighed right along with me. "You're right, Friday. She's starting to get to me, too. Don't worry, though. It's in a good way. So far." I reached down to scratch the dog's ear and he let go with another doggy sigh. "Do you want to open it?" I asked.

She eyed me suspiciously. "Are you asking Friday?"

I rolled my eyes for effect and held out my hand. "In that case hand it over if you know what's good for you."

Maddie ignored me. She was starting to do that a lot. She fished in the drawer for an opener and came up with my Buck 110. "Now that's a real pig-sticker."

She flipped open the blade and sliced through the paper before handing the envelope over. She didn't even look at it.

I was tempted to do the same until my curiosity got to me. What was Boyle passing on? Was it something about Andrea's murder? The lab report, perhaps? I wouldn't know until I got the nerve to look.

"Come on, Jim. Open it. Don't keep me in suspense."

I unfolded four pages. The first two concerned Diana's criminal record. She had quite a rap sheet. After seeing it, I wondered how she could have made a career out of the DEA.

Who did she know?

The next two pages summarized her arrests as a DEA officer. A short paragraph contained information about her mentor throughout her career. It was Kara. From the very beginning.

Kara saw to it that Diana had a career job in the DEA. Every one of her successful assignments had been overseen by Kara.

Now I knew why Diana never mentioned anything about the woman. Why she was so reluctant to let me see Kara's file. Why she kept her mouth firmly shut whenever I mentioned Kara's name.

She had a lifelong career because of the woman. And even though she was long gone, Diana's advancement hadn't slowed. Every case she worked was bigger than the one before. She was loyal and conscientious.

All of which meant that whatever was going on between her and Nicolas was business. Funny business. Was she working him? How would that turn out now that Bobbie was involved?

Diana's latest case concerned mafia and drugs and disappearing bodies. Did that mean Nick was involved? She was meeting with him. Or did it refer to something else?

Maddie sat on the desk. Leg swinging. Kicking me. I forgot she was in the room. I folded the report and placed it back in the envelope.

"So? What's up? What's in the envelope? What are you keeping from me?"

I handed it over. No secrets. "Take a look for yourself and see if you can come up with anything. Please. It's new information, but I can't figure it."

"Come on, Friday," she called. "We have homework."

She handed the envelope to the dog. He took it and pranced up the stairs to the apartment, tail wagging furiously. Maddie followed.

Maddie left me strict instructions. Get out of the building and leave her alone to figure things out. Research, she called it. She shooed Friday out with me. A pair of hang-dog looks graced our faces as the door closed behind us.

"We've been told, dog."

I ended up in front of Diana's building. Friday

looked from me to the building and back. It was old and familiar ground for him, too.

"Well, dog, here we are. Do we go in, or do we walk on by? You get to make the choice this time."

If she was even home. My choice was to walk on by. Friday's leash tightened. The dog was steadfast on the step. It was obvious he wasn't going to move until I tried the buzzer.

So I tried the buzzer.

My familiar voice over the intercom received a warm greeting. The door opened promptly and I made my way upstairs accompanied by Friday. Unlike the last time, he seemed pleased with himself that he didn't have to argue with me to get to the woman's door.

My phone pinged. I took a quick look. Maddie already had results.

Diana was involved in the case against Pilar. a junior investigator. her report was partly responsible for finding the information to pin a terrorism charge on Pilar making her guilty of terrorism

Just the information I needed. Not.

thanks I think

Trust Maddie to come up with it.

you're about to walk into her place, aren't you?

She could read me a mile away.

yes but don't worry your faithful companion is guarding the hen house

I figured that would hold her for a while.

someone better be. if either of you show up at home with her stink on you

I should have known better.

you're cleaning your gun as we speak aren't you?

I turned the phone off and advanced with Friday at my side. We met Diana in the hall. Impatient. Harried. Huge dark circles under her eyes gave away sleepless nights. I wanted to know why. What was bothering her all of a sudden?

"You brought a bodyguard. Do you think you'll need him?"

"You might be the one needing a bodyguard when I get finished with you," I said.

The look on Diana's face wasn't a happy one. "The file you wanted is on the coffee table."

I ignored her. I wanted answers. "Why didn't you tell me you were an investigator on Pilar's bomb case? Why was she railroaded, even in death? Whose bright idea was it to declare her a terrorist bomber? Who were you covering up for? Was it Nicolas senior? Was it someone high up in the DEA? Another of the three-letter experts with a failed terrorist bomb threat case who needed to make good?"

The woman wouldn't look at me. She was in it up to her armpits for someone else. But who? "Talk, woman. Your pay grade depends on it this time."

I must have gained a measure of her trust during the visits that preceded this one. Hell, maybe even all the way back to Diamondhead. She began slowly.

I sat for hours. Listening. Sometimes interrupting. Urging her to keep going. She paced the place from small kitchen to living room and back. Stopped only to make fresh coffee. Poured refills.

She hesitated and halted too many times to count. Going back and forth between cases. Only minimal descriptions for others. Some of them I knew, because I worked them. Others I had listened to the briefest of information from Kara.

The woman couldn't stop. It was turning into a long night. Friday was settling in on the floor in front of me. He seemed to know it would be a long one, too. He wasn't keeping a single eye open.

Maddie needed to know what was up. I pulled out my phone and turned it on.

the woman is spilling her guts we might be a while

as long as that's all she's spilling take all the time you need

see you soon friday misses you already he knows he's stuck with me for now

well someone has to look after you in that den of iniquity i found some new information for you

That sounded promising.

i'll look at it as soon as I get home

you'll be looking at me when you get home if I have anything to say about it

what will you be wearing?

No response. She knew by now when to leave well enough alone. Come to think of it, so did I.

Friday got up. Gave himself a shake. He was restless. He walked back and forth to the door, finally settling by it. He looked hopeful. He wanted to take care of some of his own business.

"Friday needs a walk to do his business. We're coming right back. Don't go anywhere."

Diana made her way to the sofa and finally sat down. She sighed and stretched out, as though needing rest. And perhaps she did, the way she'd unburdened herself. "The keys are on the kitchen counter. You can let yourself in."

Were it not for Friday, I wouldn't be moving a muscle. It wasn't the best place in Diana's narrative to be departing, even if only temporarily. She was beginning to get to the latest on what was happening with Nicolas and the meetings they were having.

It would wait until I got back. Provided she didn't change her mind about spilling her guts.

We exited the building. A white van slowed to a stop across the street. No one got out. Friday ignored it and went searching for a fire hydrant.

I didn't bother with the van, either.

17

Friday finished his business in short order. He had to sense how much I wanted to get back to Diana's for more questioning. In my case, it was more listening. The woman couldn't shut up. Who would have known that her old *my house, my rules* routine she handed me in Diamondhead could change so easily to *shut up and listen?*

So I shut up and listened.

I commanded Friday to heel. Scuffling echoed off the walls across the street from the T-intersection that was Diana's street. People coming out of a bar. Too much to drink. I carried on toward the intersection.

Car doors slammed and tires screeched, replacing the scuffling of boots and shoes. Now I was interested. Friday, too. Ears perked up and he tugged at the leash. I forced him to heel and we quickened our pace.

We made the corner. Everything appeared normal. No sounds of drunken puking. No passed-out bodies. The van was gone. We continued on our way. I pulled out the keys and fumbled until I located the correct key on the ring. It slipped easily into the lock.

I pushed the door open and released Friday's leash. He bounded around me and ran outside.

"No, Friday. This way." I held the door for him. He came in, reluctantly, a lot slower than he ran out. At the elevator, he made to tackle my pant-leg again. This time, to pull me out. I wrestled him into the elevator and up we went.

"Friday, you're a good old dog, but you need to learn restraint."

Like I'd be the one to teach him that.

"Okay, so maybe your mistress can teach you."

I didn't really think that would happen, either. Friday bounded down the hall toward Diana's apartment. He scrambled through the open door and came running back.

"What is it, boy? What's going on?"

I knew I closed the door on the way out. I did it twice, because I had to go back in for the keys she offered.

A mess of tipped over chairs and scattered papers lay on the floor. The thick file on Kara was missing. When I left, the woman was on the sofa. The living room was empty. Diana wasn't in the bedroom. I knocked on the closed bathroom door before entering.

Empty.

Damn. It had to be the sounds of a kidnapping I heard in the street. No wonder Friday didn't want to go up. He knew the woman wasn't there by her scent in the street.

Well shit. 911 was first to enter my mind. I

considered all the questions I'd have to answer once they hauled me down to the station. I put that on the back burner.

I didn't have any DEA numbers in my phone. And even if I did, I didn't think I'd be calling them.

Nicolas came to mind. The two of them had been meeting. Maybe he had some answers. But I didn't call him, either. I wanted to see him in person.

A quick text to Maddie to let her know I was headed home. Friday knew the way. He wouldn't allow me to reign him in. He ran hell-bent all the way. At the door to the building, I had to halt, winded and gasping for air.

Friday wasn't having it. He barked, insisting I let him in. He bounded up the first flight and halted at the office door. It was closed, as usual.

"Friday. You sure know how to make a man feel old. She's not in there. She's upstairs."

He sat at the door and wouldn't move. I unlocked it and took a quick look. Satisfied, Friday rushed the rest of the way upstairs. Finally, at Maddie's door, he began barking furiously.

18

I thought it strange, given the noise Friday was making. Maddie should have showed up to open the door. "Maybe she's out. Stop fussing, Friday."

But she wasn't out. Or if she was, it wasn't because she wanted to be. Maddie said she'd be doing research on her laptop. She had texted about it while I was at Diana's, and I was looking forward to seeing what she gleaned.

I slid the key in the door and opened it. The place was a mess, just like Diana's. Someone, possibly the same characters, had been here, too. If she was missing, Maddie had to have been number two on the kidnapper's list.

Friday was beside himself. He ran from room to room. Sniffing. Searching. Finally barking. I ignored him. Not wanting to make the mistake I made with Bobbie, I looked in the closet. Some detective I proved to be until I remembered we walked past her car on our way from Diana's.

Bobbie was already Nick's captive. While she wasn't being held against her will, I was certain she was a prisoner just the same. Call it the Stockholm syndrome, but she wasn't getting out of there on her own any time soon as far as I could tell.

Now Maddie was missing. I could only assume she was in the hands of the same people who took Diana.

I called to Friday. The dog's barking didn't quit. Already I was loading my automatic. I hammered the mag home and slipped the action, preparing to stick my head past the door frame to check the hall. I caught sight of Maddie, coming my way. She gripped her pistol in both hands. Friday stopped his barking and ran back and forth between us, tail wagging furiously.

"Where the hell have you been? I've been going crazy wondering if you were kidnapped, too."

"Too?" She looked at me quizzically and reached behind to holster the pistol in the small of her back.

"Diana is missing. Friday needed to go out. When we returned, someone tossed her apartment and hauled her off in a white van. When I saw this mess, I thought you were taken, too."

Maddie looked around the apartment. Her laptop was gone. The power cable was still plugged into the wall, stretched to the max. Whoever wanted it pulled it straight from the jack, in a hurry if they suspected we'd be making our way here from Diana's.

"Damn it. I had all kinds of new stuff I wanted to show you."

"I'm glad you're safe," I told her. "I was worried." I put my arm around her while she continued looking around the apartment.

"I heard them coming. With so many feet pounding up the stairs, I figured it was time to skip. I looked out the window to check if it was SWAT. I didn't have time for anything but the pistol. Lucky I was even dressed."

She sat up on the counter and looked at me. Friday sat at her feet. He had to be wondering something, too.

"Diana spilled her guts for so long I thought I was going to have to book a room."

Maddie didn't look so happy.

"She and Nick are up to something. She wouldn't tell me about it, but it involves the business out in the swamp. She's been working with him, going out in the boat. I'm pretty certain it's drug-related. How it fits, I don't know."

"Have you heard any more from Bobbie?"

My answer was a simple one. "No."

I left it at that, unsure how Bobbie was involved with Nicolas.

If someone knew Diana would be spilling her guts to me, they'd need to get her away. If someone at the DEA discovered she was secretly taking files out of the office, that would be trouble enough right there. I didn't think the outfit would be up for kidnapping their own agent. I was pretty sure they'd be more likely to SWAT her and take her in.

That left Nicolas. He had been meeting with her regularly. He took her out on his boat on numerous occasions for meetings, according to Bobbie. Something was up.

"Get changed if you need to. We're going sightseeing in the everglades."

Maddie left and returned wearing a ball cap.

"My kind of woman. What would it be if we were

going out for a spur-of-the-moment dinner instead?"

I was trying to keep it light. It might not be so light when we found out what was waiting for us at Nick's place in the swamp.

"I'm sure you'll find out eventually," she said.

19

I was pretty certain Nicolas wasn't wandering around the swamp without a firearm. Most likely, he had more than a few. I made sure Maddie had extra ammunition for her five-shot, and then considered my own bag of tricks. I nixed that idea right off. Surely an AK and a couple of magazines would be overkill.

Maddie's look of concentration was something I never saw before. "The drive out to the swamp is going to give you too much time to think, Maddie. Try not to get too wound up. Keep your eyes open. Keep an open mind. If you're not prepared to pull the trigger, don't aim your firearm at anyone."

She was thinking already. "I can't help it. The trips to the range didn't prepare me for this eventuality."

"It's normal. You can stay behind if you want." The words barely left my mouth before I knew it was the wrong thing to say. The woman was determined not to leave me in the lurch.

"I'm coming with you. What kind of partner would I be—"

We headed for the car. Friday, sensing something was up, made sure to be first out the door. I tried herding him into the office, but he refused to be decoyed. He halted only long enough to look up at his mistress with an expression that seemed to say, *I'm not having any of this nonsense*. Or maybe it only seemed like it.

The dog rushed past us, hurried down the stairs, and waited impatiently at the bottom.

We got on the road, and Maddie fidgeted for the first ten minutes. A knee bounced in an effort to displace nervous energy coursing through her body. In the back seat, Friday stuck his head out the window like a biker in the wind.

"I feel sick," she said, and rolled down the window to imitate Friday. Her short hair fluttered in the wind. Friday barked his approval. My voice rose to be heard above the noise.

"It's normal. Saying so won't help, but it's true. You don't know what to expect. We'll find only out what's coming at us when we get there. It could be a freight train. It could be a walk in the park."

I might not believe it, but Maddie seemed to. She settled back in her seat and closed her eyes. Her fingers drummed the dash as she began a rhythmic beating to an incomprehensible tune.

"Don't stop talking, Nash," she said. "I'm listening. Whatever is playing in my head isn't making sense. Can you tell?" She halted her tapping.

I changed the subject to one she was familiar with by bringing up her nemesis. "Diana's kidnapping couldn't possibly be DEA. I'm pretty sure they would use SWAT to take her down for an arrest. We did some of that when I was contracted to them. To my knowledge it wasn't done to actual agents very often."

"So you're thinking it was Nicolas and company in the white van? Why would he go to all the trouble?"

Exactly my question, too. "Perhaps he realized Diana knows too much about what he's doing out there. Remember, they met up on numerous occasions. She was probably enabling him. Maybe wanting information and evidence on what was really going on. Who might be involved."

"Did she tell you anything when you were talking to her?"

Not so much.

"She talked around it. I think she was scared she might say too much."

"Well, she must have said too much. She's in the back of a van with a hood over her head on the way to nowhere."

Maddie was learning.

"I have no idea. Maybe her place is bugged. It's too late to take the time to know for sure."

She looked across at me and grinned. "Bugged? Film at eleven and I promise I won't shoot you. Partner." I wasn't about taking any chances. Sure, Maddie was smiling, but I knew the woman was jealous of Diana, even if she wouldn't admit it.

"Nothing to see there. Just the good, old-fashioned crying session while she spilled her guts. Besides, good old and faithful Friday was keeping an eye on me."

"Yeah. And you're lucky he can't talk," she said.

Good boy Friday seemed to have a second sense about Diana and how the woman affected me. I wanted to tell Maddie he kept me honest in Diana's presence twice now. It wasn't the time, not when we were on the way to the glades and trouble.

A lull in the conversation allowed me to turn my thoughts to Bobbie. How deep was she in with Nicolas? Had he turned her to his advantage? Or was she being a steadfast holdout, capable of collecting the evidence she was so certain she'd find?

After seeing her on Nick's turf, I wasn't convinced she was still on our side. She had quite happily climbed onto a tabletop and danced up a storm with another of her swamp buddies. She appeared to be in awfully deep with Nicolas and at least one of his employees. Role play gone wild, maybe.

Still, I believed she was doing her job. Play loose. Play fast. Play for keeps. Find out who killed her friend, Andrea. She was out for revenge. She made that plain enough.

The woman had already seen me do something similar. I let it happen with Nicolas senior. I sat by and did nothing while an alligator made mincemeat out of the man.

Maybe that's part of the reason we were headed back to where we started after that deal went bad.

But for one thing.

It hadn't gone bad. How could it? Nicolas senior ended up right where I wanted him. Dead. That he disappeared into a hungry alligator's stomach was in no way an inconvenience.

I wanted to know who in the state police I should talk to about my suspicions concerning Nick. I tried calling Don Boyle back in the city, but there was no signal. Then I remembered reception at this end of the swamp was spotty. Bobbie's delayed texts barely made it through. I tossed the phone on the seat.

We were on our own.

Maddie, on edge, withdrew into herself. She went silent. Refused to look at me. Kept staring out the window. Even Friday couldn't budge her. He kept trying. Nudged her with a cold nose. Eventually, he gave up and went quiet in the back.

"We're going to have to park and walk. Will Friday be able to stay?"

"I can't leave him in a hot car."

Great. Then why not leave him back at the office like I wanted? "It's shaded where we'll be stopping. Will that be enough?"

"I'll roll down the windows and leave a door open, but he's not staying inside. He knows if he gets too warm to get out. We've done it before. I brought his water, too. I'll put that out for him."

She reached back to tug at Friday's ear. He was all about sitting up, tail wagging, happy his mistress was paying attention, finally.

I pulled onto the trail and parked. It was near where I last saw Bobbie. The small promontory was deeply shaded by plenty of leafy vegetation.

"Friday should be good here, Jim. It's shaded and cool," she said. Maddie brought out the water bowl, filled it, and placed it on the ground next to the car. Friday sat down beside it.

"Friday." The dog looked at her, expectant. Stood up on all fours. "Stay."

He obeyed and sat and we made our way to the end of the trail. I looked back, not quite believing my eyes. "He's still there."

Maddie halted and gave me a look that would melt an iceberg, as though I wasn't quite nuts but well on the way. Her hands went to her hips, elbows cocked, as if she was about to lecture me. "Of course he is." She grinned. "All the men in my life do what I tell them. Now come on."

The attempt to suppress her grin failed, forcing her to turn and tromp off. I made sure not to let her stay ahead of me.

"All the men? Just how many are there?" I wanted to know.

I didn't wait for an answer. I passed her and took the lead.

I led Maddie to the bushes where I hid out on my last visit. It was a convenient and familiar observation point. The spot worked well in the dark of night. A fresh look in daylight made the sparse cover unusable.

A vehicle approached at high speed, engine racing. Raised a cloud of dust on the gravel road. We crouched and the off-white van bounced past. It swayed precariously from side to side as tires slipped in the sand and gravel. The driver wrestled with the wheel. The van looked to be a match for the one I saw in the street the night before.

It halted with brakes locked. Tires skidded in

sand. The impatient driver leaned on the horn. Two males exited and hauled a woman with a black hood over her head out the rear doors before slamming them shut. I recognized Diana.

"That's her, Jim."

So did Maddie.

"How do you know?"

"Big tits and long legs. How else?"

Smartass.

Diana struggled against her captors, attempting to delay the inevitable. She twisted and bent and stumbled and fell. All for nothing. Manhandled. Pushed. She ended up dragged to the wharf and a waiting swamp boat.

The aircraft engine started in a cloud of blue exhaust and ticked over, idling. Diana was dumped aboard and fell into the flat bottom.

The noise drew Nicolas out of the chickee. He rushed to meet the men. Arms waved in a lengthy, animated conversation with Diana's captors. He gestured down the road in the direction they had come. Satisfied, he untied and climbed aboard. The throttle advanced, and he steered the boat at low speed. Clear of the docks, he firewalled the throttle. The boat took off with a loud roar.

My best guess was that he was headed for dry land. He'd dump Diana and wait for the gators to line up for the feeding frenzy.

No mess. No fuss. No bother.

I knew, because I allowed it to happen to his father, Nicolas senior. Our threesome had faced the business end of Nicolas senior's automatic in his drunken stupor. We lived to talk about it when a kindly gator wandered ashore and dragged Nick, struggling and screaming, into the marsh, never to be seen again.

In my estimation, Nicolas had to be planning the same thing for Diana. As a swamp dweller like his father before him, Nick would know how alligators felt about meat fresh for the picking.

20

I was anxious to get going. If Bobbie was still here. If she hadn't run off again.

Maddie tugged at my sleeve. I shook her off.

"Jim—"

She didn't get the message. I ignored her and went to move forward.

"Jim. Wait."

I hesitated. "Now what?"

She couldn't have missed the exasperated tone of my voice.

"I took a look at the online map before we left. There's a storage shed. In back, in the bush. It looks like a warehouse. Rows of stacked steel drums run from behind the souvenir shop to the shed. By the look of it, they're up on some kind of elevated platforms.

How old was the image she looked at? Would they still be there? Did it even matter?

"Steel drums? Are you sure?"

Gasoline drums, probably. A fuel truck would come in to fill the drums. But why no tank? Surely that would be more convenient given the number of visitors and rides in the boats.

"That's what they looked like in the photo. I zoomed as close as I could. I can't figure it either." She shrugged.

"Well, let's get it in gear. We're burning daylight."

Maddie looked at me like I was playing a part in an old western. Given her age, it was one she would never see. It was my turn to shrug before going on. "Bobbie's last text said she was in the house. I think we should start there."

Loud voices drifted across the clearing. It was the men at the dock. One wanted to get out of Dodge. The other thought it would be a bad idea. It kept them occupied. We kept to the side of the road. Used the sparse vegetation for cover. We halted at the chickee to watch and listen. There was no sound from inside. Together, we entered. Moved silently from room to room.

No Bobbie.

We regrouped and observed the men still on the dock. One of them went into the gift shop and returned with a pump shotgun over his shoulder. He walked onto the dock where he joined the second man from the truck.

"What the hell are they doing?"

We had our answer when the second boat fired up in a roar of blue exhaust and settled into an idle. The men began loading the boat.

"Drums. What do you think is in them?"

"Drugs, maybe. Or worse." I didn't say what might be worse, and Maddie didn't ask. I was thinking bodies. The boat headed off at full throttle. I used the distraction to check the small of

Maddie's back.

"You feeling me up or checking for a gun?"

"A bit of both. If it wasn't there I'd get you out of here so fast your head would spin. You'd be back at the car with Friday."

"Whatever you say, boss. What's that?"

She pointed at a long bit of cloth drifting across the road in front of us. The brightly colored scarf was caught on a stalk of swamp grass. The familiar scarf fluttered in the breeze.

"She has to be here. Where? Where could she be?"

Just because the texts stopped coming couldn't mean what I thought it could. It had to be a function of a bad signal. Or—

There it was again. I wouldn't allow myself to think about it for even one second. Bobbie had to be here. She had to be.

"Wait here."

My voice was filled with desperation. I left her and made my way back to the chickee. I climbed the steps to the rear of the house. It was where I remembered the bedrooms to be. Bobbie's bag would be in one of them. I searched frantically and came up with nothing. I returned to Maddie, still crouched in the bushes beside the road.

"Did you see anything?" she asked.

I shook my head.

"That can't be good."

I pulled the burn phone out and dialed Bobbie's number. It rang, but there was nothing but silence surrounding us. The phone had been destroyed. Or the battery was dead.

"We're out of luck and on our own, sunshine.

There could be more of them."

The door on the van slammed shut. It sped off in a cloud of dust and sand toward the main road. Both boats were out of sight in the swamp. Now we were truly alone.

"He's going to leave Diana the way we left his old man." Gator food.

"What do you mean? When?"

Now was not the time to explain. "We need to find Bobbie. I don't think she was in the van."

"I didn't see her either. She must be here somewhere."

Maddie ran for the scarf. Fingers moved to mouth to sound a loud, piercing whistle. In seconds, Friday was bounding toward us, leaving his own small cloud of dust as every paw kicked up sand and dirt. He skidded to a halt beside his mistress and sat down. Ears perked and he looked up.

Maddie balled up the scarf and held it in front of the dog. He rubbed his nose and sniffed and stood up. His tail swished frantically.

"Find her, boy. Find Bobbie. Go."

Friday took a final sniff of the scarf and bounded off. He criss-crossed the front of the compound. Not satisfied with that, he headed for the house. Maddie followed and I left them to continue the search.

The souvenir shop was empty. I looked inside the trailers for anyone. They were empty, too. Everyone had been given the day off or they were out in the boats with Nick.

I made my way back to Maddie and the dog. They were busy investigating the trailers I just left. One in particular he halted at, waiting. I'd already looked inside. Maddie opened the door and Friday headed for the bedroom.

That answered one of my questions. I took a second look. Found Bobbie's bag in the closet. It was filled with clothes. Was she moving in, or preparing for a way out? I shooed the dog out and closed the door.

Maddie regarded me. "It looks like she moved into it at some point."

It was impossible to hide the look of disappointment. Maddie pretended not to notice, but I knew. She ignored me while Friday continued his search with Bobbie's scent fresh on his nose.

Bobbie had to be here. But where?

In the distance the roar of a swamp boat grew closer. It had to be the returning kidnappers. Nick ran his boat aground beside the dock. He left the engine ticking over at idle and jumped out, swinging a shotgun over his shoulder. He made for the souvenir shack.

I observed Maddie and Friday moving to the edge of the clearing. She kept busy with an eye on the dog as he worked, nose to ground, still on the search for Bobbie. His tail wagged frantically. He raised his snout to test the air. His tail halted, seeming to need to concentrate all his efforts on the search for a scent of his quarry.

Nick must have known we were there. Maybe a camera. Maybe Diana. The shotgun racked and Nick rushed out from between the outbuilding and the souvenir shack. "All right, Nash. Where's the woman? Get her on the road beside you."

The shotgun was too close for comfort. It would do a lot of damage if Nick pulled the trigger. Maddie came out from behind the bushes. She ended up in front of me, directly in the line of fire. Unlike his drunken old man, Nick's grip on the shotgun didn't cause the muzzle to waver in the slightest.

Maddie took it upon herself to keep in front of me. That wasn't where she needed to be, and it sure as hell wasn't what I wanted. Shielded from Nick and the shotgun, I reached behind my back. I gripped the pistol in my belt and stepped out from behind Maddie in one motion. My other hand reached for her belt and yanked her out of the way behind me.

I raised the pistol. Took single-handed aim. Pulled the trigger. Nothing. I dropped the useless automatic and yelled.

"Shit. Maddie. Get out of the way."

I grabbed for her again. Kept myself between her and Nick's shotgun. Forced her to turn around. I scrambled to get a grip on the handgun I knew to be tucked into her belt and came up with a handful of shirt. I cursed, fumbled, and came up with the five-shot. My other hand shoved Maddie, trying to force her to the ground.

She cursed.

I cursed.

She went down.

Why Nick never pulled the trigger through it all, I'll never know. I wheeled around, both hands on Maddie's weapon. My grip tightened. Nick's shotgun boomed.

Maddie scrambled for my useless automatic. I

kicked it toward her, willing her to stay on the ground. "Keep behind me, woman."

She mumbled something incomprehensible and started to get up. I kicked her knee. She collapsed against me and fell to the ground. The handgun wavered. The shotgun boomed. Bits of sand and gravel and buckshot scattered in front of us. Maddie rolled to the side. I grabbed the back of her jeans and heaved her behind me one more time.

"Stay put, dammit."

Maddie fumbled with the automatic in a vain attempt to clear the jam on the unfamiliar handgun. I struggled to keep a grip on her as she attempted to get into a crouch to take fruitless aim at Nicolas. I wasn't having any of it.

Nick racked the shotgun. It boomed again. We were saved by his refusal to shoulder the thing and take proper aim. I prayed to the gods and brought up Maddie's revolver.

Nick realized his mistake as he stared down the muzzle of the stunted .357. The butt of the shotgun reached his shoulder. The muzzle centered in slow motion and got a lot bigger as it found its target.

I got off two rounds from the five-shot. One of the magnums found a home and raised a puff of smoke when it penetrated Nick's left shoulder. He slumped. Hung onto the shotgun. Still intent on his mission. Unbowed. Unwilling to surrender. He brought it up one more time with his good arm.

Out of the corner of my eye I witnessed Friday. He cleared the road at full gallop and became airborne. His aim was good.

I couldn't chance hitting the dog. I stood,

unmoving, with the handgun aimed at Nicolas and now Friday in mid-lunge.

Nick began slipping to the ground. Friday was almost on him. In what seemed like slow motion, the dog connected with his shoulder. The ferocity of Friday's charge and his weight spun the man around. Nick finished the turn, tripped on his feet, and tumbled the rest of the way.

Friday landed beside him. Rolled away. Frantic legs flailed as the dog struggled to get up. He halted on top of Nick, growled, and bared his teeth before looking at Maddie. A subdued Nick didn't move a muscle.

Maddie commanded her dog. "Watch him, Friday. Good boy. Good boy."

Nick's good arm and hand inched its way to the shotgun. At the same time, he tried to sit up. Friday backed off. His jaws moved to grab an arm. One-handed, Nick racked the shotgun. Friday's jaws connected. His head shook like he was chomping on a play toy. The shotgun boomed. Overhead, pieces of palm frond fluttered to the ground.

Resigned to defeat, Nick released the shotgun. It slipped to the ground. Sensing the man's distress, Friday backed off. Immediately, he sat on the shotgun and remained beside Nick, on guard and ready.

"You all right, Maddie?"

"Hell, yeah!" she exclaimed. "Good shootin', pardner."

She fumbled with the jammed automatic, freed it, and fired two rounds into the ground to check her work. Nick winced as brass bounced in his direction.

"Now it works." She handed it over and I returned hers.

"Keep us covered, Maddie. I don't trust mine."

Nick's labored breathing had me concerned. I didn't want him to die here. Blood covered the front of his shirt. I bent to check for a pulse, even though it was a shoulder wound and a scattering of Friday's bite marks. He'd live. I moved to pick up the shotgun. Friday refused to give it up.

Maddie called to her dog. "Friday. Come. Heel."

She slapped her thigh and the dog obeyed. He didn't heel, though. I think he took it as a sign that he needed to start the search for Bobbie all over again. He disappeared beneath the underbrush. Loud barking started almost immediately.

"I think he might have found Bobbie. Where the hell did he get to?"

Friday bounded into view, barked, and jumped back into the brush. "You go, Nash. He knows you now. I'll stay with swamp boy."

I wondered if Bobbie thought I might kill the man, but I didn't give it further thought when Friday returned. He made for the house and then passed it to make for the shack on the dock. I was about to change course to meet him when he did just that.

The dog backtracked to halfway between the buildings and made for the row of steel drums Maddie described earlier. He walked the rows, sniffing and snuffling. He halted suddenly and then sat down and waited for me to catch up.

"Good boy, Friday. Is she in there?"

The dog's tail wagged frantically. I banged on the

drum hard enough to wake the dead. A faint voice greeted me.

"All right, boy band. That's more than enough. I'm in this one."

Bobbie couldn't be so bad off. "I'll be right back. Don't go anywhere. Friday is going to stay with you, okay?"

"Where the hell am I going to go? Who's Friday? What took you so long? Where have you been? Was that gunfire? What's happening?"

I went off to find a wrench. I passed Maddie on the way. "Go let her know I went for tools to get her out. She was too busy asking questions to listen."

"How on earth is she breathing?" Maddie asked.

"Whoever put her in there left the bung uncapped."

I returned to find Maddie at the drum, praising Friday and consoling Bobbie by reassuring her she hadn't been deserted. Even Friday was woofing support and wagging his tail.

It took time to unfasten the clamp ring with the wrong tool. With the cover finally off, Bobbie crawled out of the drum on all fours. She collapsed to the ground. Friday took it upon himself to give her a nuzzle with a cold nose and a consoling lick to the face.

"Who's this?" Bobbie asked.

She squinted and pushed at the dog's face. He changed tactics and licked her hand. Finally, he sat and waited for a treat for doing his duty and rescuing the woman.

Maddie handed out one and then another. "Good boy, Friday. We couldn't have done it without you.

I'm going back to the car. I'll try to get a signal and call the state police and an ambulance."

Friday looked up at me and hesitated before following his mistress. He lunged away, wagging his tail until I couldn't see them in the underbrush.

I helped Bobbie up and she leaned on me for support. "Who was that?"

"That was Friday. He helped find you."

Bobbie looked skeptical. "Not the dog, Nash. The woman," she insisted.

"Have I got a story for you when it's time to catch up. Let's get to the dock. The EMTs will be here to collect your buddy Nick. Come on. They'll be waiting for us."

Maddie's car and Friday were out of sight.

"It looks to me like your friends are part-time."

"They'll be back with the cops in tow. I need to pick someone up. Do you want to come?"

"I'm not staying alone in this shit show to wait for cops to show up. Get me out of here."

Sirens and police cars arrived while we made good our escape into the swamp before we would be forced to answer questions.

"What are we looking for?"

"Diana. I think Nick might have put her off at that same island where Nick senior intended to kill us."

We didn't have far to go. A patch of clothes struggled on the ground as our noisy boat approached. Diana wriggled and managed to stand up. She was happy to see anyone, even me. Without saying a word, I cut her free.

She looked from Bobbie to me. Maybe she was

even grateful as she climbed into the boat for the trip to the dock.

Conversation was limited to yelling and shrugging over the engine noise. There'd be too many questions to answer. I wanted to get them ashore to talk to the police.

The state police took our statements. I made arrangements for Diana to get back to the city. I didn't know it then, but that would be the last contact I'd have with Diana Holbrook.

My own unhappy duo would be in the swamp a while longer as we laid out what we thought Nicolas junior had been up to.

21

Bobbie and I agreed to return to the state police office when requested. We climbed into a cruiser to be chauffeured home. The drive was made even longer by Bobbie's silence. I had too many questions bubbling just below the surface. I wouldn't be asking them just yet.

Still, I had a pretty good idea what transpired. I chose not to force her to get defensive and angry. Hell, I was just as guilty with Maddie, although Bobbie didn't know that. Yet.

I remembered the first time I watched Bobbie sliding across the seat for the ride out to the everglades. I remembered Andrea, too, and our time together. She was with me when we went to rescue Bobbie the first time.

Once in the city, we were dropped just past the spot were Maddie usually parked. Her yellow car was missing. Upstairs, Friday's water bowl was missing as well. I checked beneath the sink. His food was gone. I wandered downstairs to look in the office. His bed and the second water bowl was gone.

Maddie's empty holster lay on the desk. It was the

one I loaned her when I hired her. It sat on top of a folded piece of paper. Tired and depressed, I tucked it all into my desk drawer without thinking about it.

Water splashed in the shower. I closed the bedroom door and hurried to change the sheets and make the bed. There was enough to explain without dragging Maddie into it now that she had up and disappeared on me. I was becoming accustomed to the women in my life disappearing.

Or worse.

I determined to tell Bobbie about all of it, the sooner, the better in my estimation.

Bobbie was cold and distant when she came out of her turn in the shower. I knew right off she needed room, and I'd be the one to give it to her. I packed a bag and let her know I'd be staying down the street at the boutique hotel. She could see me there if she wanted.

We agreed to meet at a small restaurant down the street from the hotel. Bobbie didn't ask a lot of questions. Maybe she didn't want to know. I had a few of my own, but I didn't ask, either. There was no point. After all, she headed off to Alaska at the end or our last gig. There was no reason she couldn't do the same again.

I let her know I was glad to have her home, safe and sound. I even suggested we get a dog.

Right out of the gate she said no to that. I should have known better.

That I hadn't seen the texts she sent from the glades until it was almost too late never came up. I didn't push it. She didn't, either, but I sensed there was something bubbling away beneath the surface.

We would talk eventually. We'd have to, but it would be when we were both ready. I tried a couple of times to ease her into it, to no avail. I even went so far as to suggest counseling for both of us.

She turned me down flat. That's when I knew our relationship was on borrowed time. I began preparing myself emotionally.

I began taking long walks in the early evening. Sometimes I'd head to the beach and grab a burrito and a coffee and sit looking out over the water. On one of my excursions I thought I recognized Maddie and Friday on the beach, far in the distance. The woman was tossing a Frisbee, and what looked to be a black dog was madly wagging his tail and retrieving it.

The dog must have caught a scent. He froze and looked, tail wagging ever more furiously, if that was possible. The woman turned to follow her dog's gaze.

I stood and waved frantically, hoping she'd recognize me. She brought up a hand up to shade her eyes and turned in my direction. She changed her mind and turned back to the ocean almost as fast. I made a point of going back to look many times. I never saw the pair again.

It took Bobbie a couple of months before she eventually settled in to where we were before she disappeared. I was afraid she'd head off again, the way she had up and gone off to Alaska the first time. I was prepared for the eventuality.

Maybe our relationship was growing.

I stopped looking out over the beach for Maddie

and Friday. Maybe I was getting over them, finally, too.

An envelope arrived in the mail. I figured it was Diana. No return address. Photocopied papers convinced me that the father of Kara's son, James, turned out to be Kara's handler.

The handler convinced Kara to complete one final assignment before she resigned, thus the disappearance on board the Saskia. She hadn't wanted to do it. She threw caution to the winds when he convinced her it would be the last. Her life with me would be guaranteed after that.

Kara would never know how long I looked for her in that ocean of water. It sucked every remaining bit of pride and anger and life out of me. I turned to drink for months before I gave up and resigned myself to her death.

When she finally reappeared with what I thought was my son on board a renamed Saskia II, it brought it all back. My new wife, Pilar, doubled down and took matters into her own hands. That was when I knew I was truly free of Kara. My only promise was to James and his aunt, Erica. It involved finding out who his true father was.

With that done, it was over once and for all.

Even the death of Pilar's killer was anti-climactic as far as it went.

More months went by. Bobbie and I settled into something unnamed as far as relationships go. Finally, she admitted she'd been accepted as a first officer by a regional airline out of Iowa. She packed her bag and boarded a bus.

I was alone again.

Eventually, Boyle showed up with a coroner's report on Andrea's death. Even better, he was carting the oil painting Andrea did for the office. They picked up a man, and were grilling him as we spoke. Apparently, Andrea ended a relationship with a bartender where she worked. He was jealous as hell that she left the bar and started working for me.

I hung the painting where it belonged, and Boyle pointed to a fingerprint in the oil paint. It was something I noticed, and remembered thinking it was Andrea's, and that she'd cover it before the oil paint set up and dried. I never bothered mentioning it.

Boyle picked up on it in a search for evidence while we were down in the dumps over Andrea's murder. He was about to walk out before he stopped for another look at the impressive painting. That was when he saw the print. It was the reason for hauling it off to the station.

"We tracked another man down and we're in the process of extraditing. I know how much that painting means to you, but I'm going to need it when it comes to trial."

He asked after Bobbie and Maddie, and I had to tell him I didn't know where they were. We commiserated about police work and women and how tough it was to have a life with a cop.

"We need to go fishing, Nash."

"And we will, Boyle. As soon as I get my head straight."

I leaned back in my chair and put my feet up on the desk. I was feeling reasonably good about everything. Well, okay, truth be known, almost everything. Nick senior was disappeared in the glades. Nick junior would go away for threatening Diana, a federal agent. Miscellaneous characters on the fringes would get some time, too.

And then there was Andrea. Her killer had been captured thanks to the painting she did for the office.

It turns out life works in strange ways, and there is justice, one way or another. Who could know that a simple poke at a painting could have such life-changing consequences?

The sun was about to disappear behind the buildings across the street. The unlit neon sign was throwing a shadow across Andrea's painting on the opposite wall.

It was Bobbie who talked me out of anything fancy with the sign. *Stick to basics*, she told me, if I remembered right. Priority one would be a new sign. Until it arrived, I was stuck with the old.

I looked over at the door. It would need new gold leaf. I'd make the call first thing in the morning.

It seemed like some semblance of equilibrium had been restored in my world. I locked the office and headed up the stairs.

I n two weeks, I had the new sign. Simple. Direct. No nonsense. The lettering on the door matched. I turned the sign on and went down to walk across the street to check it out.

JIM NASH – INVESTIGATOR

The sign looked pretty good.

I climbed the stairs to the office. I hit the space bar and brightened the laptop's dim screen. I pulled up the word processor, chose a font, and went to work.

The finished product looked good in page view. Satisfied, I sent the document over the network. The printer hummed and spit out a single page.

HELP WANTED
Inquire within

PX DUKE

A FRANK ROSS BIKER TALE

NO WAY OUT

La línea is behind biker Frank Ross when he breaks down at a casino on the west side of the Salton Sea. There aren't many options for a place to stay, and Frank isn't happy to be there until he meets a reformed stripper. Frank's happiness soon turns to despair when he opens her closet door. Pick up an e-book or a print book to find out why Frank is up to his neck in trouble.

About the author

Peter Duke is a Canadian author. He resides and writes in a small college town in Southern Ontario.

Aviator. Motorcycle rider. Vagabond. Drifter. Trouble-maker. Jack of all trades and master of none. Peter Duke has been riding and writing about the places he's been and the people he's seen for many years. Some of his writing is factual; some of it isn't. He likes to leave it up to readers to imagine the lies that could be the truth.

https://pxduke.com

peterxduke@gmail.com

Check out all six books of the Harry Delaney Adventure series. Learn why Harry makes his way from the North African desert to the Mexican Baja. Discover why he ends up having a triumphal return to the deserts of North Africa.

Available in e-book and print.

Jim Nash Read Order

Marina Mystery
Twisted Sisters
Sleeping with a .45
Pirate Cay
Thrill Kill Jill
Greetings From Key West
Lost Paradise
No Angels
Mexico Gamble
No Picnic
Fallen Angels
Vendetta
A Girl's Best Friend
Dead End
No Harbor
Dog Days
Startup Blues

Last Stop to Nowhere / The Last Goodbye
Revenge Is Justice
Escape
Wedding Bell Blues
Breakdown
Little Girl Lost
Forget Me Not
All The Glitter
Mexico Time
Partners In Crime
Shop Till You Drop
Lobo
No Free Ride
Gone
Stealing America
Blame It on Djibouti
Trouble in Paradise

SEASONAL

Trick or Treat
Helping Santa

OTHER

The Snap Brim Fedora Caper
The Lady in White
The Lady in Yellow

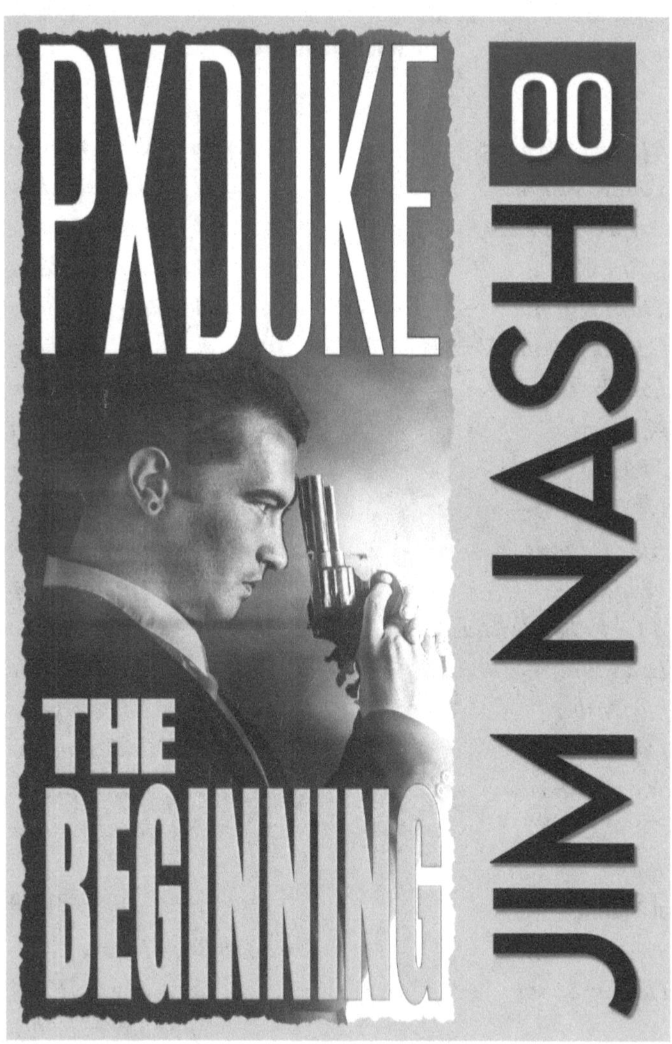

Police Detective Jim Nash has a murky back-story in the police department of a major city. Check it out.

Print books

Jim Nash

Jim Nash The Beginning
Gun Crazy
Gun Crazy 2
Gun Crazy 3
Fallen Angels
Last Stop to Nowhere / The Last Goodbye
Revenge Is Justice
Escape / Forget Me Not
Wedding Bell Blues / Breakdown
Mexico Time
Lobo
No Free Ride / Gone
Stealing America
No Escape

Harry Delaney Adventures

Dead Reckoning
Uncharted
Go-Around
Sand Storm

Frank Ross Biker Tales

No Way Out
Bank Robber Dames
Bad Girls

Other

The Last President